FED FROM THE BLADE

Tales and Poems
From the Mountains

E D I T E D   B Y

CAT PLESKA
and MICHAEL KNOST

Woodland Press, LLC

Published by

WOODLAND PRESS, LLC

www.woodlandpress.com

Copyright © 2012, Woodland Press
ISBN 978-0-9852640-5-5

Copyright © 2012, Cover Art by Cat Pleska

SAN: 2 5 4 – 9 9 9 9

Each of the author contributors to *FED FROM THE BLADE* own the individual copyrights to his or her work, but each has given Woodland Press certain literary rights making it possible to assemble their writings, along with others, in this anthology.

DEDICATION

Fed From the Blade is dedicated to Sunday at 2, my writing group. Thanks to Karyn, Lynne, Michelle, and Paul for their inspiration and their belief in my writing. They keep me grounded in the reality of life and in the narratives I create each time I pass to them new writing.

ACKNOWLEDGEMENT

My heartfelt thanks to: co-editor Michael Knost for his advice, my husband, Dan, who helped me with all aspects of the project, Belinda Vance for her assistance with the cover art, Jerry and Lynne Barker for their hard work organizing the submissions, West Virginia Writers members who sent such good writing, and Keith Davis for his kindness.

FED FROM THE BLADE
TABLE OF CONTENTS

INTRODUCTION

West Virginia, what an extraordinary place it is, as is all of Appalachia. And our land is known for its many storytellers continually bringing forward their enriching tales. I was excited to be asked to edit an anthology for Woodland Press, and to extend the call for what I knew would be wonderful stories. But the challenge that followed! Who could have guessed we would receive 170 submissions? This became one of those moments when it is hard to accept the reality of limits—to select stories knowing that practical constraints play their role in any book, including this anthology. I read and read, without knowing who created each piece of art because I was president of the organization whose members were submitting and I wanted to be fair.

As I considered the entries, a certain kinship among the stories developed. Not a similarity in style, as each author's work in this project carries a distinctive voice, but a sort of reaching out across the ether to one another, some sensibility, a bonding as to tone, or mood. And in the end, I chose based on these sensibilities.

This spirit of kinship led to a feeling of cohesion. It always does. For me, selecting works for this anthology meant finding a connection to link poems, fiction, and nonfiction because I wanted these eclectic stories, as diverse and as different as the individuals who wrote them, to jive in a book.

I am making this sound as if it was a smooth and easy process. But there was struggle especially when we needed to name this anthology. My fellow editor, Michael Knost, and I couldn't seem to agree. Fortunately, one night we were witness to a reading of the poem, "I am the Daughter" by Sherrell Wigal. And there it was: the title, pulled from a line in her poem, which is included in this anthology. Perfect!

So dear reader, celebrate with us this diversity of offerings. Allow yourself to be drawn to the characters, the settings, and the circumstances. Submerge yourself in the imagery, the lan-

1

guage, the humorous and dark stories, the spooky and paranormal, the tragic romance, the drama, the rejoicing, the heartbreak, but what is most important, the tale well told. This collection represents the tip of the iceberg concerning the writing talent, in this case, amongst members of West Virginia Writers, Inc.

Enjoy!

Cat Pleska, *editor*

I Am The Daughter

By Sherrell Wigal

I am the daughter of old men,
fiddlers born in 1890,
who climb stage stairs without assistance
and tap their feet in perfect time
to their own tunes;

Lone, aged men who frequent
any cafés that still exist
to drop the quarters and corny jokes
onto scrubbed chrome countertops;

Old men in green pants,
white shirts, black shuffling shoes
and brown suspenders.

They are my fathers all,
white haired, hairless, hatted men
with eyes the color of every rock
I ever touched.

I am the daughter's daughter
miles and years removed
from one aged man, who sliced
green apples with a pocket knife,
fed me from the blade, and left
before I learned his tunes.

Splinters

By G. Cameron Fuller

From where she stood next to the barn, she could see acres of alfalfa in the valley. She knew how the grasses quivered when the wind moved across them, the shifting browns and purples of the ripened grains. The raspy soft sounds the stalks made as they gentled against one another. But these were memory; there was no wind blowing today. She told herself maybe it was better this way—that much less to miss if she had to leave.

Out of breath after her walk from the house, she leaned one-handed against the barn wall. It seemed so long since the quarter-mile walk had been effortless. Her knees hurt. The rough wood under her palm made her remember she'd have to take her hand away with an upward motion or risk splinters. The barn had been on the farm for as long as she had, and had been badly beaten by the seasons, especially the winters, when it was barely used, and never cared for. She breathed slowly and deeply, watching her breath sift out.

Where the forest started the grasses stopped, unable to grow in the shadow of the trees. She could still see well enough to make out the dark treeline. This time of year the trees cast scant shadows, but this time of year nothing ever had a chance to grow. Winter was even worse. At least that's what she used to think, how she used to think about it.

She had never cared much for winter, in fact liked it less as time passed, although she hadn't dreaded it in the last few years. Not like she used to. Each year the barren season seemed shorter. Probably that was because her husband had also been getting older: less restless, less urgent, age had softened some of his edges. Still, winter had meant long days and longer nights. If they had had children, everything might have been different—no, it surely would have been different if they'd had children. She didn't blame him, but he never got over it.

Winter was downtime on the farm: no work except the feedings, a few repairs when weather permitted, and towards February, usually some wood chopping. He'd put on his coat and say, "Choppin' wood is good for two warmings—once when you chop it, once when you burn it." He always thought that was very funny. She'd heard it several times a season for forty years. Over and over. She just sighed. At least he could work it out on the wood for a change.

Never allowed to help with any of his chores, she mostly spent winter indoors, doing crosswords or making him soup or cooking the canned vegetables and venison that was their standard winter fare. She wondered if anyone would help her out by giving her some venison next year, but then remembered she had never cared for venison, not really, not anymore than winter.

If she was allowed to stay—which she doubted—the real difficulties would be with the field below. Maybe she should have waited until after he brought in the harvest; he would've eaten the soup just as eagerly in two weeks. She could sell all the livestock, except maybe a milk cow, possibly give them to Elton for coal and a few eggs every week. But that field . . . she couldn't just let it lie fallow. That would be a waste. Maybe she could hire the Loughery boys, or the Colebanks to put up the hay; they would probably be willing to come around now. She could tell them to sell the hay and keep fifty percent.

She leaned against the barn, thinking nothing after that. Nothing, for a very long time.

Her face was numb and her eyes watery by the time she decided she'd better call the sheriff. Get it over with.

She forgot to lift her hand as she took it away from the rough barnwood and winced as she felt a splinter break off in her palm. She would take care of that as soon as she got back to the house. Even before she called the sheriff. Splinters fester if not removed.

Christmas Cards

By Kathleen Furbee

Just off work, I come barreling down the highway late that night, and came to the curvy part of the road out on the Pike, when I seen this wobbly light in the road. I didn't have time to figure out whatever the heck it was. I didn't have time for nothing. The next thing I seen, the very next split second, was her blue housecoat come sailing up over the hood, and then her eyes, big surprised old lady eyes, bigger still with the bifocals attached, look right into me, in that split second that lasts forever, before the crash. She didn't make no sound, no scream, just a thud. I hit a deer one time and it was a lot like that, on that road even. But the deer didn't look at me. It busted through the windshield, just that fast, and flew past my head and laid thrashing in the backseat. Tore up that car. I had to go call the cops to come put it away, and the game warden come out too, to get it out of there. The old lady though, once I got stopped, once I got skidded off the highway down over a bank and into a tree, with my engine killed but the headlights still shining off kilter and crazy like, well, the old lady just hung there, outside the car, pinned between the car and the tree, a big oak I crashed into. She drooped all limp with blood draining out of her like all those deer that were tied to about every vehicle in the county in the past month of hunting season, their eyes glazed over and blood dripping down the side windows, or in the truck beds, and under the tailgates.

She was dead. There was no doubt about that. I jumped out of the car, out the passenger side cause my side was busted in, and worked my way around to her. I learned CPR back when I was a nurse's aide, but I couldn't figure a way to do it there on the old lady. I couldn't get to her, pinned like she was, although I did try. I grabbed ahold of her arm and tugged and pulled, and the only thing I got done was yank the blue housecoat off her arm, and leave the arm laying out there in the cold. A little cotton nightgown was all she had on underneath the housecoat. It was real faded and worn. I tried to cover her back up. Dumb I guess, but I couldn't just leave her there all bare-armed and half naked.

I didn't know what to do. I felt dizzy like, and sick to my stomach, and I puked up all the hot dogs I ate for my supper at midnight. I felt so shaky and weak. So I sat down, freezing all of a sudden, and surprised myself by thinking about work. I work at Walmart as a soft lines processor, which means I hang up clothes on hangers all night. It's not a bad job, easier on my back than nurse aiding ever was. I sat there and wondered if I did that last box that come in, and I wondered about my evaluation coming up, whether or not Sally would give me a raise. I'd got off early, 4:30 a.m., and it made everything seem different, made me have to think it all back over, wondering.

Maybe I wondered a long time. Maybe it wasn't no more than a second. Time gets messed up sometimes, when thing like that happen. I come to a little bit, figured out this was no time to be worrying about work, and started worrying about what I should do. My husband had been after me for a long time to get me a cell phone, but it was just gonna be one more bill to pay, and I never got around to it. I wished I had listened to him for once. I'd wished that a lot in the past year. All the fussing he always did at me, I was starting to see was for my own good.

I got up and went back around to the passenger side of the car, climbed up-hill through the door, and tried to find my coat. I had cigarettes in the pocket. I'd been trying to quit. Seeing your husband suffocate to death of the emphysema kind of takes the fun out of smoking. I needed the calm of my cigarettes at that moment though. But my cigarettes weren't there. My coat wasn't there. Then I remembered how I'd been in such a hurry to get out of the store and into my nice warm bed at home I'd left the coat hanging in my locker.

Well, there wasn't nothing I could do but climb up the hill and hope some other pre-dawn soul would be coming home from or going to work and would stop when I flagged them down. Getting up the hill was tough. Steep, and stickery. There was some snow laying in icy patches, and some just starting to fall out of the sky.

8

There was some beer bottles hidden under the weeds and I turned my ankle on one, cussed, and thought about how my life had changed so much since Frank had died. I never used to cuss. I never used to do nothing but hurry home to fix his supper or haul the kids or whatever. It's funny how life gives you lots of episodes. Not just episodes, like in the soaps or something, but whole new shows. I felt like I'd been some actress playing in a movie, a good old standard mother role, like June Lockheart maybe, and then they'd put the makeup on me and turned me into this tired old woman climbing up a weedy bank in my Walmart smock in the middle of the night, and cussing.

I stopped to catch my breath when I got up to the road. I thought my chest was going to bust I was breathing so hard. I wanted my cigarettes bad. I breathed in deep and the air had that winter smell, clean and white, like every sin you ever had would be forgiven, as long as the clean was in the air. Snow was still falling, but lightly, like it wasn't going to amount to much, and down towards town, way down the mountain in the distance, Christmas lights was still lit on some of the houses. I thought of the crowd of people coming into the Walmart, hauling away those boxes of lights with that look on their faces, impatient and the kids all snot-nosed and crying. I used to work days, seasonal, but after Frank died, when it didn't matter that I wasn't home to fix his supper, when it didn't matter that I was home at all, that's when I switched to nights. The girls thought I was a crazy fool, giving up a day shift job. Maybe I was a crazy fool. Sure did feel that way, shivering out in the cold.

After I was breathing a little better again, I went over to where the crash had happened. There was a little bit of blood on the road; I could see in the light you get used to seeing by at night, the night light Frank always called it, but the blood was mostly covered with snow. The old lady's flashlight, a big Coleman kind, was smashed where I'd run over it. I picked it up anyway but of course it didn't work. Scattered around in the road was a bunch of white envelopes, like big Christmas cards. I gathered up the ones I could find and stuck them in my smock pocket. I looked over to where the car had went off the road but you couldn't tell it had even happened. If I'da died too no one would ever have known it until daylight, and in mid-December there's sure not much of that. Which brought to my attention that it wasn't at all daylight at that moment, and if a car did come and I didn't get out of the road I'd get my chance to go flying like the old lady had.

Up the hill over the road was a little frame house with the lights on. It was the only one around, and I figured it must've been where the old lady had come from. I walked up the rocks dug into the hill for steps, holding onto the metal railing there. Flower beds, empty and dark, lined the house when I got up to it. I thought about the old lady out there puttering in the summertime. I thought about how there wouldn't be no more summertime for her, ever again, unless they got that in heaven, and since Frank died, I wasn't so sure about heaven no more anyway. I got to the door and waited a minute. I thought all of a sudden about, what if the old lady had some deaf old husband snoring away in there. Maybe I'd scare the life right out of him and I'd done enough killing for one night. The thought of the old lady's eyes, big in her glasses, staring at me gave me the shivers. Made me almost puke again. I yoo-hooed loud as I could and opened the door.

The living room was cozy, tucked in with quilts and those afghans like old ladies like to make, bright colored ones with lots of oranges and yellows. There was a framed picture of Jesus on the wall, the same brown-haired, blue-eyed picture of Jesus I had on my wall at home, the one Frank liked to make fun of. It used to make me mad when I was a girl, when I married Frank, and he'd tease like that. I'd been raised up strict in a Baptist house and God was a serious thing. Frank though wasn't hardly serious about nothing, especially religion. Hunting, maybe. That was his religion. Oh the venison I had put up for that man. Every year, deer after dead deer. Oh the blood that was on my hands.

I went through the house sort of quickly, looking for family. There was just the four rooms, counting the bath with the old fashioned kind of tub. I thought of that frail old bird climbing in and out of that thing, how she might've fallen and hurt herself, and no one around would know. Least when she'd died she'd had me to look at. The bedroom was empty—no man sleeping there, and the bed was made up neat like she was expecting guests. My housekeeping had fallen off some since Frank died. There was some days I never even made my bed. That would've scandalized my mother, and me too, back when Frank was alive. But Frank wasn't alive, only I was alive, and all of a sudden I felt like I was the last living woman on the planet. Maybe the nuclear bomb had fallen, or the Armageddon had come, and I was left to deal with it all alone. At least the old lady could've had a cat, I whined to myself. Even I had a cat. I don't know what I would've done, coming home alone at night, late like this after work, without him there twining around my legs. I wondered how the old lady did it. I wondered if she got lonesome, up on that hill, with winter coming on and no one but the wind for company.

I passed the telephone, the old heavy black dialing kind, sitting on a wood stand in the hall between the rooms. I thought about calling the EMS then, but I figured, what was the hurry? Whether they came sooner or later, it wasn't going to change anything, and I wasn't yet ready for all that excitement. Maybe the old lady wasn't in a hurry neither. I thought about her hanging out there in the cold, just her and the night and that big oak tree. Maybe she needed a little time to say her goodbyes before they carted her off and put her all alone in the icebox, which was what they called the morgue at the hospital when I'd worked there. I'd took many a dead body down there, days and nights, alone lots of times. I've wrapped some bodies in my day. Cold old blue bodies and the nurses would put the toe tags on and tell me or some other aide to do the dirty work, wrap 'em up and tie the jaws and wrists and what not. Deliver them to the ice box, on their way to the hereafter. When I was younger, before I had the kids and got tougher I used to cry at night after every dead body, and Frank would hold me and say there there and call me his baby.

I went into the kitchen, feeling hungry all of a sudden. Feeling like Goldilocks, but I didn't find no porridge. Just a quart of skim milk, in a plastic jug in the fridge, and some vanilla wafers in the cupboard. My favorite kind of cookie, too, but I buy the other brand. I fixed myself some and went into the living room, and settled myself into the old lady's stuffed chair. It was warm there, right beside a gas space heater, the kind Frank used to complain about all the time. It was his job for awhile with the gas company to go around to the old houses and check to see if they were safe. Everyone used to have those old stoves.

Over in the corner of the sitting room was a ceramic Christmas tree, the kind that lights up when you plug it in, only it wasn't plugged in, and it was kind of dusty. I felt like that about Christmas this year. The kids had come by and put me up a tree, got me an artificial one so it wouldn't make a mess, and decorated it with gold balls and ribbons. If it wasn't for them doing it, I sure wouldn't have bothered. Frank was the one that loved Christmas. I looked at the picture of the old lady's man, smiling out of an old frame on the stand by her chair. The man looked to be about sixty some maybe, like Frank would be now, but the picture was old, the clothes in it from a long time ago. I wondered if he had loved Christmas.

I put my feet up on the foot stool by the chair, kind of like my footstool at home, and pulled a soft worn quilt over me. It was cozy, and I wanted to sleep. I thought about the old lady doing that, night after night, and wondered how many years it had been, how many nights she had done just that, sat there and snoozed, like I did at home. I never used to do that when Frank was alive. Even after the kids was gone, there was always something, some thing to attend to, some place to go. Now though, now when I got home from work and took off my smock I just settled down in my chair, just like here, just like here in this chair where the old lady sat, making curves in the stuffing that fit me, too. The old lady's curves fit around me like they was made by my own body. It seemed like the chair was still warm from her, and I thought about the rest of her, hanging out in the cold. It made me shiver, and I pulled the quilt up close.

I squished myself farther down in the chair, and when I did the cards I'd put in my pocket from the road poked at my side. I pulled them out, and saw one was tore open and wet from the snow, and marked with a tire track and a smear of blood. I took it out of the envelope. There was blood on the nature scene. Mountain pasture with deer. I'd bought some like them at the Walmart, on sale with my discount back in October. I was still late getting them out this year though. In fact I'd been going to finish them when I got home from work this morning. I wondered what they'd think, the ones that didn't get the cards from the old lady this year, whether they'd wonder, whether they'd notice. Inside the card said, "Merry Christmas. Love, Genevieve," in spidery old lady handwriting.

I yawned and closed my eyes. The refrigerator hummed, steady and low. And the gas stove hissed, just slightly. It sounded familiar, the same quiet as what I listened to night after night, the same soft sound of nothing and no one at home. I might've slept then. I might've not. I was in that place, that in between place, that's not here and not there, that's not sleep and not wake, that's someplace in between the dream and the real. I sighed, and the wind sighed, and outside the snow fell, just lightly, cold on her face, and soft.

Puddles

By Karin Fuller

It was easy to tell who the winners were. They lingered in the stands and at the pay windows. Talking loud. Back slapping. Dad was somewhere among them. I studied the wager board, tried to calculate our winnings, but it was beyond my grasp. My home schooling, which was necessary to limit exposure to germs, had gradually lessened over the years. Once I entered my teens—teens I'd never leave—we wordlessly agreed that structured studies weren't the best use of my time.

The breeze was playing with several old bet slips, twisting them into wobbly circles that batted against my right wheel. I was well entranced by their movement when the smell of sweat, cigarettes and beer yanked me from my brief bliss.

"Fancy chair you got there," said the man. "How fast does it go?" He stepped in front of me. Squatted down. Clumps of greasy hair poked from beneath his Budweiser cap.

"Leave me alone! My dad'll be back any second." Except it came out, *"Eee mmm-lo! Muda bubaa ne-ekk."*

Budweiser shook his head. Looked at his buddy. "Shame," he said. "Lady pretty as this."

His friend stepped around. Looked me over. Shrugged. Baggy Jeans laughed. Smacked his friend's shoulder. "Grab the backpack and let's go."

"Oo-aaa mi!" Translation: "No, that's mine!"

Bud grabbed the strap of my backpack and slung it over his arm. I tried to watch where they went, but could only turn a little before my head support blocked my view.

"Ep! Ep!" I yelled weakly, but there was some kind of commotion over at a cashier's window. People were yelling, others ran to see what was up.

My meds are in that bag. Dad's nitro. My I.D.

My suctioning equipment.

The realization triggered a familiar thickening in my throat. I

15

heard myself gurgle.

This is it. I'll choke. Dad will get back just in time to see me turn blue again. And then, I reassured myself, he'll do his thumping trick and it'll be enough and I'll be fine—again. Dad to the rescue. Always Dad. My throat relaxed just a little. Just enough.

Coming here had been a fluke. Dad had gone to the bank to close our account so the tax man wouldn't grab what was left. Sitting at the table, he finger-dragged his hair, staring at a mess of 20s and 10s and a few rumpled 1s lying on top of a newspaper. I flashed my laser pointer to get his attention.

"All the money we have in the world, right there," he'd said. "Might last another few months, but after that..." He looked to where my laser dot hit the paper. Sat up a little straighter. Swept the money off the newspaper.

"The last races of the season are at Churchill today. Maybe it's a sign. What you think?"

My smile probably looked more like a grimace, but Dad knew.

"That's my girl!"

Dad got a stranger to help lift my chair into the trunk. We'd had to sell the lightweight several months ago. We should've sold the fancy one instead, but back then, I could still drive it.

Dad insists it's a temporary setback, but muscles don't un-atrophy. It's been easier for me to accept than for him. If I'd died as quick as predicted, he wouldn't have this financial nightmare to deal with on top of everything else. The only pain involved with my disease is watching what it's doing to Dad.

There are times I wish he was more like Mom. Sometimes, I wonder if he wishes he could run away, too. I think I might be relieved if he did.

"You okay, honey?" A woman was squatting in front of me now. Sensible haircut. Practical shoes. A teacher, I guessed.

"Where are your parents?" she asked. "Can you talk?" She wouldn't understand if I tried, so I shook my head no. Dad could still understand me, but even he had trouble sometimes.

"You need help? Can I search your chair for I.D.?"

I tried to nod, but my head tipped too far forward and wouldn't go back. Drool spilled onto my lap.

Crap.

The woman straightened me, dried me. Sent her husband after security.

"They're probably all at the pay window," she told him. "Must be a fight or something." She turned my chair to face the mural of all the jockeys who've won the Derby since 1875 and began telling me its history.

Should be the horse's pictures up there, I thought. Wished I could say. I liked that she talked like she got that I'm in here. Like I'm not just a shell.

I heard sirens. One was an ambulance. That sound, I knew. The other was probably a police car. Then two.

I wished Dad would hurry. I distracted myself by trying again to calculate how much money we'd won, wondered if that was the cause for the commotion. Our pot was that big.

The last race, we'd bet nearly everything on a long shot named Lacey's Puddle Jumper. Dad said it was fate. He'd nicknamed me Puddles long ago because there is a bonelessness to me that makes me hard to lift. He said I'm like hugging a puddle.

"Think she's abandoned?" Security asked. "How long's it been?"

"Over an hour," she said.

That couldn't be right. Dad hadn't wanted to leave me at all, but it had been too crowded at the windows for my big, awkward chair. I struggled to look around, but the way I was turned, all I could see was the mural.

They began talking in hushed voices. I strained to hear.

"No ID at all."

"Too crowded to notice."

"Happens more than you think. Caretakers get desperate."

"Calling for another ambulance. That one's not for her."

"Some old guy. His heart."

I felt my throat thicken. I gurgled. Gasped.

Prayed.

Please don't let *some old guy* be Dad.
Please let him have run.
Please.

Time and Change

By Llewellyn McKernan

Here's your body, stretched out
on the lawn, stiffening to iron.
Once you rocketed down green hills, and
when I called, burst through thickets
with the speed of a bomb.

Your neck, stretched now to tighten forever—
I used to press my nose to its blond ruff
as we sat together on the porch steps,
me inhaling your baked-earth bouquet
while you listened, still as a vase, to unheard
high-strung music, your black muzzle
soft as a rose in the glowering dusk.

That nose, sentry now to dust,
was once some dark instrument that quivered
with wild carrot odes, mousse-mouse suites:
A whole orchestra of smells, intricate
as a Bach chorale, fleckless spit lying
on your lolling tongue, where a strange birthmark
reigned, shaped like California.

I imagined that music
as I walked, leashed to the collar
about your neck, and you barked and pranced,
proud as the sun that shone so vividly
above us. I pull on that collar now
but you are inmovable. I look you in
the eye, but you don't look back, those
gold-rimmed irises liquid as tears, now
gone dry and glassy.

The life that sparked them, where did it go?
Who poisoned it without a trace? Might as well
accuse the moon and stars as a dog killer
who leaves no mark, no clue to tell me who he is
or why he hated you so much?

As for me—when things got bad
and I didn't want to live, I would look for you
and there you'd be: Sitting on the porch
and viewing the yard as if even the grass
had its own charm. I would fling
my arms around your neck, rail and wail
against time and change. You'd turn your head
away. Your animal embarrassment
at such a maudlin display
made me grow calm.

But now, bone-grief has turned that calm
to stone. Reliving again and again what's past
and gone is an empty cup when
you're starving for water.

If You See Buzzards

By Wilma Stanley Acree

If you see buzzards,
it must be spring.
High above the hills.
they soar on thermals,
their wings a *V*.
You see dark silhouettes
with wing tip feathers
spread like fingers,
an illusion of beauty.

Close to a buzzard,
you see ugliness.
Wrinkled red head
too small for his body,
hooked yellow bill,
short red legs,
chickenlike feet
too weak to kill.
If you say *buzzard*,
human noses sniff
 in disgust.

If you see buzzards,
trees bud into myriad greens
interspersed with yellows
and reds, here and there
the pink of redbud,
the white of dogwood.
If you see buzzards,
you know that Persephone
has emerged from darkness.

If you see buzzards,
you see God's recyclers:
a body devoid of breath
feeding one that breathes,
a body that breathes
cleaning the land.

Garbageman Stan

By Frank Larnerd

The world is a dirty place.

To have order, you have to put things where they belong. Without that rule, everything turns into chaos. The worst thing is trash. Trash is everywhere; broken, soiled and unwanted. If you don't get rid of it, it's going to pile up. That's why I became a sanitation worker. I like to put things where they belong.

When I was a kid, I would organize everything: race cars, blocks, even my mother's make-up. It would make me nervous if my blue shirts were mixed with my red ones. Sometimes, I would stay up all night worrying if my sneakers were pointed the right way. Doctors call it "obsessive compulsive disorder," but my mom would just say, Stan just puts things where they belong. I think that sounds better.

After I graduated from high school, I tried to figure out where I belonged. I wanted to be like my dad and fit into the example he had made for me. On my nineteenth birthday, I joined the Marines, just like he had.

I was made for the Marines; they have a place for everything. The strict regimen gave things a sense of order. No. It gave me a sense of control. I was making order out of chaos. Some complained, but not me. I adapted to the rhythm of a soldier and excelled at it, until the war started.

They put me on security detail guarding checkpoints, checking cars, that kind of thing. Inside, I felt I was doing my part, cleaning up a dirty world.

One day, just after sunset, a little hatchback came flying down the road toward the checkpoint. I followed the protocols and signaled for them to stop, but they kept coming.

I didn't want anything bad to happen. I was only trying to maintain order.

After the shooting stopped, everyone was shouting and cheering. We ran to the bullet-ridden car with our rifles pointed. It had driven off the road and crashed into a ditch. One of the doors was blown off and smoke billowed from the engine. The car's windshield was spider-webbed, pocked with bullet holes. As I got closer, I could smell burning oil and blood.

There were four kids inside. Just teenagers like me. The most dangerous thing anyone of them had was a hairbrush.

In the report, my CO said the car was full of explosives and that it had been a suicide attack. They said I was just following orders and gave me a medal.

I started feeling like I didn't have control anymore.

After I was discharged, Mom told me to come home. I booked a flight and she was supposed to pick me up from the airport, but she never came. I waited for three hours and then called Dad. He left work at the plant to come get me. The whole way home he complained about Mom's absent mindedness, but when we saw the sheriff's car in the drive way, I knew he would never talk bad about her again.

It was a drunk driver. This kind of thing happens all the time, but I couldn't make any sense of it. I started thinking there was no order, no great plan, just chaos.

I started feeling like I didn't have control over anything anymore. The feeling stayed with me, even after Mom was buried. I wandered, I drank and I got into trouble. I was falling, devolving into chaos while doing anything I could to ignore it.

It made me angry, and I lost jobs and friends. I didn't care where things went anymore. I didn't care about anything.

When the drunk who killed Mom was found stabbed eighteen times, I laughed. I laughed until the tears soaked the front of my t-shirt.

One morning, I had just fallen asleep when the garbage truck came. It growled, beeped and boomed metallic thunder as it emptied the dumpster outside of my apartment. I ran out, dressed in boxers and bathrobe, my head still hammering from the night before. I was going to shout something angry and threatening.

But, I didn't.

Instead, I just watched. The garbage men seemed like ants, all scurrying and busy. Not in a bad way, but like they had a purpose, like they had order. I watched them moving down the street, hauling away stained mattresses, a three-legged table and countless black plastic bags. Before it was a dirty alley, but now it looked real nice. Somehow, the act of collecting all that chaos and hauling it away to be recycled or buried struck a chord with me.

When they had driven out of sight, I went back inside and cleaned my apartment from top to bottom. I scrubbed, I washed, and I folded. I sorted my clothes by color and organized my CD's alphabetically. In the cupboard, I grouped things by expiration date. I made sure everything was where it belonged. When I was finished, I carried down fourteen bags to the dumpster.

Looking over my orderly apartment made me feel good, like I was taking back control.

The next day, I applied to be a garbage man.

I've been working the job for over four years now and it suits me fine. My riding partner is Smitty. He does the driving while I load up the trash. We're supposed to trade off, but Smitty has a bad back and two years until retirement. I don't mind; I'm used to the smell.

I work all along route 60: Spring Hill, South Charleston and Saint Albans. There are always some things you don't expect. I've found guns, jewelry, and even a brand new microwave still in its box. Once, I found a Macho Mike inflatable love doll in the dumpster behind the church on Washington Avenue. It looked like a dog had been using it as a chew toy.

I don't judge anyone. I just do my job. I load up the junk and take it away to be buried. Only once have I ever taken anything home with me.

Number 221 Grant Circle is a pick up you can't forget. Nice house, red brick with white awning and shutters. It has a two car garage and a fenced in yard. If I had a family, I would want to live there.

The house isn't the unforgettable thing; it's Mrs. 221 Grant Circle.

I had only seen her once. It was June and we were collecting like normal. There wasn't any trash in front of 221, so I called for Smitty to pull ahead when the garage door bursts open and I see Mrs. 221 Grant Circle come running after the truck with her arms full of black plastic bags. Even with the garbage, she looked like a goddess. Her hair was honey gold and had the tussle of sleep. Flawless legs poured out from under her red silk night shirt down to her delicate feet.

She made me think of a chandelier, something beautiful and fragile. To me, she seemed to hang over everything, aglow by some mysterious power.

I yelled for Smitty to stop as I jumped down from the back of the truck.

"I'm so sorry," she said, huffing for breath.

I took the bags from her, but couldn't think of a thing to say. We stared at each other and she smiled.

At me.

I'm not sure how to describe it. I felt like I had gotten shot by one of those space ray guns that freeze you in time. Everything seemed to stop, and then the door to 221 opened and everything sped up again.

Mr. 221 Grant Circle slammed out of the house, marched down the front steps, his bathrobe flapping behind him. "Get your stupid rear back inside!"

Mrs. 221 Grant Circle lowered her head. That's when I noticed the fresh purple bruise under her eye.

"You trying to show your goods off to the friggin' garbage man or something? I said, get back inside!" I stood there with the bags and watched Mrs. 221 retreat inside the house. Mr. 221 Grant Circle glared at me before following her inside and slamming the door.

I tried not to think about it much.

Once a week, Smitty and I would collect on Grant Circle. I would look for Mrs. 221, but she was never there, just bags of trash. As I said, I didn't think about her, until I found the box. It was sitting on top of 221 Grant Circle's cans. Not in a bag, just lying broken and hidden under one of the green lids. My mom had one like it. I remember stacking her lipsticks next to it while the box played music and the plastic dancer spun.

Mrs. 221 Grant Circle's box looked special like she had had it a long time. She must have had it since she was a little girl. It was something special, that's why she couldn't cover it in black plastic.

The music box was pink with red and white flowers painted along the trim. The sides had come apart and the felt had been torn. Worse, the dancer was broken in two pieces, separated at the waist like someone had thrown it into a wall.

I'm not sure why, but I tucked the music box inside my yellow safety vest. Later, when we emptied the back of the truck, I noticed lots of bloody towels and ripped up photos. In one of the pictures, Mrs. 221 was wearing a crown and a sash. She looked like a princess except the jagged rip down her face. I crumpled up the ruined picture and left it in the rank sea of pop bottles, diapers and broken crap.

I found a place for Mrs. 221's music box on top of my bookshelf. After work, I would play my CD's and feel my eyes drawn to it. The more I looked at the music box, the more I knew it wasn't in its right place.

It stayed there for weeks, just broken, chaotic junk in the middle of all my routine and order. I thought about throwing it away, but it didn't belong in the trash either. I didn't have any plans for it; fixing it just kind of happened. I refitted the sides of the box and replaced the hinges. The pink felt wasn't hard to replace, and I touched up the flowers and added a clear finish.

Using a piece of wire, I fitted the dancer back together. I sanded down the rough edges and used modeling clay to repair little chips on the dancer's waist. The paint on her head and dress was scuffed so I decided to repaint those too.

At the hobby shop, I found a honey-gold paint for the hair and a silky red for the dress. When I was finished, the music box didn't look like trash. I'm not bragging or anything, but I bet it looked even better than when Mrs. 221 first got it.

The music box played its melody with perfect order. It made me feel good to rescue it from the chaos. Now, it just needed to be put in its place.

I didn't want to make a scene or have Mrs. 221 think I was some kind of stalker. So the next week, I slipped the music box inside my safety vest and waited until we reached 221 Grant Circle.

When we got there, I hopped off the back of the truck. As I bent over for the trash, I slid the music box into 221's mail box. Just a gift from your friendly neighborhood garbage man.

Maybe, I thought, she would like to have it back. Maybe there was even a part of me that hoped it would help Mr. and Mrs. 221 get along better.

It didn't.

The next week, I saw Mrs. 221 Grant Circle again. She didn't seem to notice me. She was digging in the garden with one of those three pronged garden cultivators. Her left arm was in a sling and her face was battered with bloody scrapes.

When I got home that night, I was really worked up. I started to blame myself for what had happened to Mrs. 221. Instead of helping, I got her hurt. My anger started to boil, and I could feel the chaos starting to close in around me. I was thinking about hurting myself when I realized who was really to blame.

The whole thing was really Mr. 221's fault! If he wasn't such a sack of crap, he wouldn't be hitting her! She doesn't deserve that!

With my rage planted, the idea started to grow. By the time midnight came, I was ready. I laid out everything I needed on the bed. I moved the items around, trying to find their proper place. Flashlight, gloves, rope, duct tape…

No. Let's try it like this: Gloves, ski mask, flash light…

Maybe: Knife, ski mask, gloves…

Nothing worked. No matter how I tried to organize the tools, I couldn't get any order out of them. They wouldn't fit, every combination looked like chaos.

A half an hour before my shift started, I put the tools away.

I didn't want to see Mrs. 221 again. I was ashamed that I might have gotten her hurt. Mostly, I was ashamed that I almost let the chaos overtake me. That would be something Mr. 221 would do.

I was so nervous the next week when Smitty pulled the truck onto Grant Circle. My butterflies left in a hurry when I noticed 221 didn't have any cans out front. I signaled Smitty to keep going when I heard a voice call out.

"Garbage man! Garbage man!"

Mrs. 221 Grant Circle was running after the truck. Her arm was still in a cast, but out of the sling. Faded bruises still showed along her jaw, but she was smiling.

"Can you help me?"

Smitty backed the truck up, and I followed Mrs. 221 to the garage. She bent over to lift the garage door, and I grabbed for the handle to help. Our hands touched for just a moment: hers perfect and beautiful, mine scarred and covered in dirt because I'd forgotten to wear my gloves. I stepped back and shoved them on.

I got the door opened, and she pointed to a large travel suitcase. There were bulges along its sides, like something lumpy was inside. A dark puddle had begun to form underneath it.

When I lugged it down the driveway, the suitcase left a long, red stain on the concrete.

Mrs. 221 started to rub her hands together frantically. She was talking a mile a minute, jumping from the weather, to politics, to her garden in the same breath. Even though she was talking to me she couldn't take her eyes off the suitcase. I heaved the suitcase in the back of the truck, then leaned in and scooted it as far forward as I could.

When I got down, Mrs. 221 held out her hand. "I'm Crystal," she said.

I took off my glove and took her hand.

It felt like being struck by lightning.

"It's nice to know you, Crystal" I said. "Make sure you spray down that driveway with bleach."

Her eyes warned of panic, so I held her hand.

"You don't want that old transmission fluid to stain."

Crystal nodded and smiled. When she turned to walk away, I

pulled the gardening trowel out of her back pocket. I didn't look at the rusty stains on it. I threw it into the back of the truck.

When I stepped up into the cab, Smitty turned to me, grinning. "You making friends back there?"

I put my glove back on and twisted the truck's mirror to watch Crystal as she walked back inside.

"No," I said, "just taking out the trash."

Last Letter

By Joshua S. Robinson

I don't know how long Ashley's ghost sat across from me before I noticed her. I jumped and nearly knocked the table over, attracting the attention of every patron in Mike's bar. My sheepish hand wave allowed the eyes of the living to return to the football game, but the eyes of the dead remained on me. She was barely more than an outline, but the sad expression on her face held me transfixed. Only when I heard chair legs dragging on the old wood floor could I look away.

Mike sat down beside me and put a fresh beer on the table. I apologized for the ruckus, then took a long swig and tried to assure him I was fine. I wondered whether or not to tell him that his little sister's ghost was watching us, but before I could decide Mike reached across the table toward her. Ashley extended her own arm, and as her wrist melted into Mike's hand she became more distinct. Shades of tan skin appeared, and the crimson of her long, curly hair. The sadness left her bright green eyes, and a little smile formed on her lips.

"I figured she'd eventually show herself to you," Mike whispered.

Stupefied, I managed to ask, "You've seen her before?"

Mike nodded. "I've been seeing her since a few months after she died," he said. "She led me to this place. You remember what a dump it was? But she kept bringing me here and I figured she wanted me to buy it and fix it up. While I was renovating, I'd see her smiling, and that's how I knew she had forgiven me."

"For what?" I asked, failing to remember any mention of an argument. Mike tended not to talk about Ashley much around me, and I was grateful for that.

Mike turned toward me, and his hand left the space where it met Ashley's arm. She also withdrew, and her presence reverted to the melancholy, transparent form I had first seen. "She wanted to drop out of college," Mike said. "As far as I knew, her grades were fine, but she told me she didn't feel like she belonged there for some reason. I came down on her pretty hard because I didn't want her to make the same mistake I did. She started crying and hung up on me, and that was the last conversation we ever had."

I tried to offer condolences, but couldn't find the words. Mike looked over his shoulder toward the crowd gathering at the bar. "I'd better get back," he said, rising from his chair. "I know it's scary, but if you can see her, she probably wants to tell you something." I watched him cross the room and casually resume his work as if nothing had happened.

I took another drink of beer, staring into Ashley's eyes—through them, really. What could she possibly want to tell me? She had said all she needed to five years ago when she refused my proposal. I didn't want to stop her from going to college, but I wanted to keep what we had going. I thought she loved me. I sure loved her.

As I drained the bottle, Ashley's ghost rose and walked toward the exit. I turned my head to watch her and noticed Mike nod in the direction of the door, encouraging me to follow his sister's apparition outside. She had traveled nearly a block by the time I reached the sidewalk, and the early afternoon sun rendered her almost invisible. I walked briskly and caught up as she turned down Main Street. When we reached the old church, she turned again and cut through the city park. The familiar trail weaved between trees that had only begun to shed their gold and scarlet leaves, and we soon emerged onto an alley I knew far too well. My stomach tightened as I realized Ashley was leading me to her parents' house. I hoped she didn't want me to confront them.

I had never felt welcome in this part of town, where the alley cut between well-manicured back yards of large, freshly-painted houses. Luxury sedans and SUVs gleamed in the sunlight as they awaited the next opportunity to announce their owners' affluence to the rest of us. Had anyone been out they would have undoubtedly offered kind greetings, but in a small town like this it didn't take long to find out what insults they muttered behind my back. Ashley's parents had put on a paper-thin facade, their disapproval of our dating poorly concealed behind forced smiles.

I sighed and made sure no one was looking before following Ashley's ghost through the open gate into her parents' back yard. She appeared less like a spirit here, and I might have been convinced she was corporeal had she not melted through the door of the old garage her parents used for storage. I checked behind the loose brick Ashley had shown me when we were dating, and the key was still there. Sneaking in made me nervous, especially during the day, but I was compelled to find whatever message Ashley hoped to convey.

Enough light streamed in through frosted glass windows near the ceiling to reveal a large, covered object in the center of the building. Ashley's ghost disappeared into the unidentifiable mass, so I pulled the tarp free to reveal what remained of an old car. I shivered as I recognized Ashley's little coupe and imagined her fear during those final moments while she spun helplessly out of control on black ice. I hadn't thought of it before, but I hoped her death came as quickly and painlessly as possible.

Ashley's ghost waited where the driver's seat had been, now a twisted chamber where no solid being could fit. She stared to her right at something I couldn't see, so I pried open the passenger door. The deteriorated hinges groaned so loudly I worried someone might hear, but no one came. Debris and broken glass lay scattered about the interior, and it smelled of oil, smoke, and ammonia. Large rust-colored stains covered parts of the dashboard and center console. I fought to keep myself from vomiting, and wondered why her parents would keep such a horrific reminder of Ashley's death.

Tears ran down her cheeks, which were no longer transparent. Her presence felt even stronger than it had when Mike touched her at the bar, and I uttered a terrible thought: "You're trapped here, aren't you?"

Ashley turned to face me, raising her hand slowly. I recoiled from the ghost's touch and immediately regretted my harsh reaction. Before I could apologize, she pointed toward the glove box. Shocked, I hesitated before opening the compartment. Papers, napkins, and other miscellaneous items spilled onto the floor, and atop the pile was a letter addressed to me.

My heartbeat boomed in my ears as I tore open the envelope and unfolded the single piece of paper it contained, my efforts hampered by shaking hands. It took only a moment to recognize the date in the upper right corner, and a warm tingling sensation ran the length of my body as I realized the words on this page were among Ashley's last. I blinked to clear my blurred vision and steadied my hands against the car to make out the writing.

It began with an apology. Ashley had thought about our relationship all the time and felt terrible about the way it ended. College was harder than she imagined, and she missed me. She wanted to drop out, but felt incredible pressure not to disappoint anyone. None of her new friends could encourage or comfort her the way I had, she wrote. I choked up as I read the last words: "I know I didn't act like it, but I really did love you. For what it's worth, I should have said yes."

My eyes filled with tears, and at least one hit the paper before I could wipe it away. I had been so angry that I cut her out of my life completely, never attempting to make amends after she left. This revelation of her true feelings knotted guilt and heartache together in my stomach. It wasn't fair. I said as much out loud, then looked toward the driver's seat. The apparition had disappeared; no explanation was coming.

Anger consumed me, fueled by the shame the letter had invoked. I tore the paper into as many pieces as I could, then threw the shreds into the passenger's seat. "I didn't do anything wrong," I fumed. "I don't deserve this." I stormed out of the garage, slammed the door behind me, and headed back to the alley. I imagined Ashley's father coming out of the house to confront me, but a glance over my shoulder revealed no pursuit. I retraced my steps to the corner near Mike's bar, then took the shortest route home. I cursed my decision to walk to town that morning, and by the time I reached my trailer I was winded and my legs burned.

I went inside and dropped myself on the couch. The room spun around me, and closing my eyes only made the couch spin instead.

I jumped to my feet and started to pace, but my shin found the coffee table, and I kicked it violently in retaliation. The walls closed in and my vision became narrower. I stumbled to the kitchen sink and splashed cold water on my face, then sank to the floor and leaned against the cabinet. Eventually, the trailer stopped moving and the rooms returned to normal size, and I staggered to my feet. I poured myself some water and emptied it into the desert that was my throat, then refilled the cup and sipped it slowly.

The memory of Ashley's ghost flashed through my mind, and I thought I saw her outline near the door. I shouted, "Get out!" and threw my cup at her, a stream of water trailing the plastic missile. But there was no target to meet, and it ricocheted off the door and onto the carpet.

I wanted to forget everything about Ashley: the way the light caught her fiery hair, how her emerald eyes shone when she laughed, the sweet song of her voice, the softness of her hand in mine, the rosy fragrance she wore. I wished our relationship had never happened, and then I remembered the old, beat-up shoebox in the bottom of my closet where I kept trinkets from our time together. I dug it out with the intention of destroying it, but as I stomped through the kitchen I slipped in a puddle on the linoleum. I caught myself on the counter top, but dropped the box. The impact popped the lid off and a few things spilled onto the floor.

I cursed and knelt to pick up the scattered mementos, but before I could shove them back into the shoebox my eyes locked onto a picture of Ashley and me at our senior prom. My mind wandered back in time, remembering how gorgeous she looked, how much fun we had together, and how the night passed far too quickly.

My chest turned to lead, each shallow breath a labor, the air coarse against the back of my throat. How could I even consider destroying this? I delved into the shoebox, photographs and little presents transporting me to days long forgotten. I read the notes Ashley had given me in the hallway at school and heard her voice as my eyes traced the curve of each large, flowing letter.

Finally, my fingers found a small, felt-covered object. I recoiled but the nostalgic euphoria had already abated. I hunted for another memento to triage the heartache, but only the little black box remained, diminutive in size but ominous in meaning. I considered reburying it beneath the joyful memories, but I knew I had to confront the token it contained. I carefully picked up the box and slowly opened it.

A tiny diamond, maybe a tenth of a carat at best, was mounted on a simple gold band that rested in the crease of a beige pillow. I pulled it free and cast the enclosure aside, enthralled by the ring I had offered Ashley on the final night of our relationship. The echoes of the argument enveloped me, and I winced as I recalled our harsh words hurled like daggers at one another. My anger swelled as I tried to temper myself against the final blow.

Shutting my eyes only intensified the vision of Ashley's resentful expression, but as I fought to expunge the memory something changed. Her eyes became dull, her countenance regretful, her form hollow. Her voice came as a whisper, reciting the final words of her letter: "I should have said yes."

I gasped as I realized her heart had been broken that night too, a regret she carried to her grave. Ashley's spirit was trapped by a memory even death couldn't erase, and had led me to the letter to ask forgiveness, not make me feel guilty. My eyes snapped open and I sprung to my feet, holding the ring tightly in my fist and vowing to make things right.

I slipped the ring carefully into my pocket, grabbed my keys, and hurried to my car. As I sped along the mile of road between my trailer and the highway, my stomach turned at the thought of revisiting the wreckage. Her manifestation had been the most substantial there, but that place evoked too violent a reaction for a proper goodbye. Instead, I drove south to the memorial gardens where Ashley was buried. After looping through the property a few times, I recognized the path to Ashley's grave and parked nearby.

I felt like an intruder, and tried to walk as quietly as possible. The cemetery was devoid of other people, but I suspected I wasn't truly alone. The biting October wind and long, imposing shadows hinted that the tranquility of this place was an illusion conceived to benefit those of us who still drew breath.

The granite headstone announced her name in cold, formal lettering that left me feeling disconnected as I read the inscription over and over. I longed for Ashley to offer a sign I was doing the right thing, like she had for Mike. "Are you here?" I asked. "Can you hear me?" She did not appear.

I called again, but Ashley remained absent. I began to doubt my decision to come here instead of returning to where I found the letter. My cheeks flushed with shame as I remembered tearing the paper to shreds, and I would have given anything to take it back. It meant a lot to know Ashley had cared about me, but I feared my anger had pushed her away again.

Tears formed as I bemoaned my actions, and I pulled the ring from my pocket. I wiped my eyes and gazed into the diamond, which glistened despite the waning sunlight. I still had no explanation for why Ashley refused my proposal, but I had been wrong to rebuke her. Maybe if I hadn't been so proud, I could have given her the friendship and encouragement she never found at college. A thousand possibilities raced through my mind, culminating with the speculation that if we had worked things out, maybe she'd still be alive.

I sniffled and scanned the area again, but saw no trace of Ashley's ghost. Wreaths adorned nearby graves, and I imagined the families who had left the floral remembrances. They probably believed their loved ones to be in a better place, but I couldn't allow myself such comfort. I knew Ashley's spirit was restless. I had failed to bring her the closure she needed.

My strength wavered and I dropped to my knees, weeping. I conceded that I would never see Ashley's ghost again. She was gone forever, and I missed her terribly. Regret fueled my mourning, and I sobbed until my chest ached from heaving. No grand gesture could undo the mistakes I had made, but I hoped that by offering a loving farewell, Ashley could somehow find serenity.

I placed the ring reverently atop the headstone so its brilliance wouldn't be concealed in shadow. "I forgive you, Ashley," I whispered. "I'm sorry I held that night against you for so long, and I hope you can rest peacefully now." I swallowed, but the lump in my throat wouldn't budge. My voice was weak and broken as I said, "Goodbye, Ashley."

By the time I reluctantly left her grave, the sun had sunk below the treeline, outlining the western hilltops with orange and pink. I had taken only a few steps toward my car when a frigid wind cut through me. I shivered and hugged myself against the cold, but my left shoulder went numb. I turned my head to see a ghostly hand resting there, wearing a ring exactly like the one I had left at Ashley's tombstone.

I wheeled about to face the apparition. Ashley smiled wide, her green eyes dazzling, her form strikingly clear and emanating a soft white glow. She withdrew her arm and placed her hand on her chest, then mouthed the words, "Thank you," before fading from view.

I tried to call after her and checked all around, but Ashley's ghost had vanished. I ran back to her grave and smiled as I scanned the top of the monument. The ring was gone.

Hallowmas

By Edwina Pendarvis

The wind blew her hair across her face as she stood on the porch waiting for Mrs. Bales to open the door.

"I'm collecting clothes for the city mission. You have anything to donate?" she asked, shivering in the autumn wind. She was thin and so pale the veins on her hands showed blue—almost as blue as her eyes, which shone through the strands of dark hair swirling in front of her face. Behind her, leaves swept through the chill night air.

"I was saving some for the church bazaar, but one charity's as good as another, I guess. Just a minute," Mrs. Bales replied, and went upstairs to find the old clothes she'd been meaning to drop off at the church. The girl turned around and stared out into the dusk. A little clown, a vampire, and an acrobat skipped through the leaves up to the house next door, calling, "Trick or treat, trick or treat!"

"Thanks very much," the girl said, holding out her arms to receive the paper bag full of wadded skirts and sweaters. Mrs. Bales watched her walk across the street to the Davis's house and ring their doorbell. The teenager didn't look like she belonged in their neighborhood, even on Halloween.

It was after midnight when the girl got home with the bags of clothes she'd collected. As soon as she stepped inside her kitchen, she pulled out a big metal washtub with a wringer attached to it. She lit one of the gas burners on the stove to heat water for the wash.

Taking a fuzzy pink sweater from one bag, a silk jacket from another, and a pair of expensive argyle socks from yet another, she put them all in the tub and poured hot water over them, singing softly as she poured.

Steam rose from the tub.

She reached for a bar of lye soap on the shelf and dropped it in. As she hummed and stirred, the clothes darkened, going around and around, like deep-sea creatures. Splashed by the soapy water, her hair lay in wet black spikes against her white cotton blouse.

Mrs. Bales looked down. Getting ready for her bubble bath, she suddenly felt hot. The skin on her neck and breasts flushed. It turned bright red and began to blister; when she pulled off her robe, strips of skin came with it. Summoned by her terrified cries, her husband rushed into the steamy bathroom just as she lost consciousness.

Walking down the hall from the living room to his bedroom, Bill Davis started hopping from one foot to the other. The soles of his bare feet were scorching. He looked down to see the skin melting away from his ankles to his toes. The purplish scarlet muscles began to show through, then they too began to bubble and melt away. He started screaming as the white of the bones appeared.

In the middle of the late night movie, Sarah Moore gasped. At first she couldn't breathe, then a rush of air streamed from her lips in a long sigh. As she lay helpless on the couch, her chest caved in, her ribs folded together in slow, silent motion, like a collapsing tent.

The girl dried the clothes, pressed and folded them neatly before she went to sleep. She delivered them to the city mission early the next day. Making the sign of the cross, the priest on duty blessed her for her charity. She smiled up at him and walked out into the clear morning air.

To Make Her Smile

By Diane Tarantini

Tawny was rolling silverware when the two of them came in. Mother and daughter. She'd watched their white Honda Civic circle the diner three times, in search of the door. She smirked.

"Smile, Tawny," Sue Ann said. "You get way better tips when you smile."

The mother tapped the point of her jumbo, rainbow-striped umbrella on the floor as she and her daughter strolled beside the row of booths. They didn't sit until they found a clean one. Tawny kept rolling.

Sue Ann bumped Tawny with her hip. "Tawny, they're in your section."

Tawny winced. "You want 'em? It's five minutes to close."

"Naw. I gotta do the bathrooms. Now get on out there."

Tawny tossed two menus on the table. "Evening," she said.

The mother beamed. "Howdy." The girl smiled too.

"My name's Tawny. The specials are on the inside front of the menu."

The mom tilted her head. "Tawny? That's a neat name. I like it."

Tawny's mouth pulled to the side. "What can I get you to drink?"

"Do you all have sweet tea?" the mom asked.

Tawny clenched her teeth and nodded.

"Oh, boy! You know you're in the south when you can get sweet tea."

Tawny turned to the girl.

"Water, please."

Tawny headed back to the kitchen. She wondered if the woman knew what her name meant. A long time ago she'd looked it up. Light brown to brownish orange. Nothing about her was tawny. Her hair and eyes were dark brown, the same color as the used coffee grounds she dumped out of the Bunn coffee maker umpteen times a day. She scooped ice into red plastic glasses. Let the tea and water overflow. Tawny wished she didn't know how she got her name.

Wished her mom had never told her. How her mom had seen Tawny Port on a bottle at the liquor store and that's how Tawny Port Blevins came to be.

Tawny had gone to the library a few years back and checked out a baby name book. Some day when she got the time she'd change her middle name to Portia. Tawny Portia Blevins. Sounds classy, she thought. Like a movie star. Tawny pulled her order pad out of her apron pocket and walked back out. The mom and girl were leaning across the table. Their foreheads almost touched. Tawny cleared her throat.

"You ready?"

The mom glanced at the girl. The girl shook her head. "Give us a minute please, Tawny," the mom said.

Tawny huffed and returned to the kitchen. She grabbed a rag and the bleach water spray bottle and headed back out to the dining room.

"Country ham or pot roast?" the mom was saying. "I can't decide."

"Me either," the daughter said.

Tawny folded the rag in half twice. She sprayed and wiped a two top and its chairs. Refolded the cloth. Squirted and swabbed some more.

Do you have any idea how beautiful you are?

Tawny's breath drew in sharply. She quit picking at the spot of dried ketchup. Again? It's been so long.

The mother's gaze was a caress as she watched her daughter read the menu. *Do you know how I dread each day coming and going? Knowing it makes the day you'll leave for college be that much sooner?*

Tawny spied on the two of them from under her lashes. The girl didn't answer. Tawny knew why. The mom hadn't spoken out loud.

It was the one thing special about Tawny—her ability to sometimes hear people's thoughts. She couldn't do it until two years ago. Until Randy drove his fist into her right ear.

That night everything seemed to move in slow motion as she crumpled to the floor. The room seemed tunnel-like. The lights far away and small. The noises all echoey. *You're nothing special. Never will be. I'd treat a good woman better. But you're not, so I won't.*

Tawny had struggled to prop herself up on her elbow. Her head wobbled.

"What?"

"Shut up! I didn't say anything. Get me another gin and tonic."

Tawny squinted over at her mom, who never looked up from her *People* magazine. She pulled herself up using the coffee table. Headed for the kitchen.

Tawny waited in front of their booth, her pencil stub an inch from the pad. The mom grinned and pointed to her selection on the menu.

"I'm going to have the pot roast, green beans, and mashed potatoes, please. I'd also like an order of coleslaw. I don't care if it's extra. I love slaw."

Tawny gritted her teeth. Nodded and wrote.

I'm sorry you're so sad, Tawny. Or mad. Are you angry at something? Someone?

Tawny didn't look at the mom. She licked the pencil tip with her tongue and faced the girl.

"Open-faced turkey sandwich please. With mashed potatoes and gravy. And carrots. Thank you."

Tawny met the girl's gaze. *Why don't you smile? You'd be so pretty if—*

Tawny snatched their menus and hurried back to the kitchen. She clipped their order on the metal strip over the grill. "Order in," she told Hugh's back.

Tawny dragged the coleslaw bucket out of the walk-in cooler and scooped some into a side dish bowl. She considered making a list on the back of a to-go menu of all the reasons why she was sad. And mad. For Mrs. Aqua Turtleneck.

She peeked out at the dining room through the lattice work. She spoke softly to herself.

"Mom moved in with me back in October when her roof sprung a leak. That's one. Randy's stalking me, ever since I dumped him.

That's two. Mom thinks I should take him back because he says he's gonna be a doctor some day. 'Cause he bought us groceries that one time. No way. I may not be special, but I'm not stupid either. Oh, and I'm thirty bucks short on this month's rent. That's three."

Tawny shoved a tray down the sideboard, for when their order was ready.

"And really, it's not that I'm sad or mad. I'm focused. On changing. The way things are. No way I'm gonna be her—*my* mom. Or Sue Ann, for that matter." She glanced around to see if anyone was listening. Tapped her breastbone and whispered, "I'm going to be different. The trick is to not make the same mistake twice. I had one kid. I'll not have another. He hit me once. There won't be a second time."

Tawny found the generic Windex. Sprayed the cooler doors. Wiped left, right. Then in circles. Faster and faster.

"Plus, I'm saving for college. Or maybe I'll do that certified nursing assistant program. What I need is a job that doesn't tank when the university's not in."

Tawny caught her reflection. Squirted the woman with the furrowed brow. Covered her with the cloth. When she was sure there were no more streaks, Tawny tossed the blued towel in the milk crate in the supply closet. *And I'll make darn sure my daughter goes to college. Like yours is going to, Mrs. Aqua. I saw her sweep the brochures onto the bench when I walked up. It was kind of sweet. Her trying not to make me feel bad.*

Sue Ann came over and wrapped her arm around Tawny's waist. Tawny squirmed away. Smoothed her apron front.

"Order up," Hugh said.

Tawny unloaded the tray, dish by dish.

The mom rubbed her hands together. "Thank you so much," she said. "It looks and smells delicious."

Tawny dropped onto the booth bench behind them and swept the crumbs and straw wrappers off the table, onto the empty tray.

"Good food. Good meat. Good God, let's eat."

Tawny fiddled with the salt and pepper shakers.

"Oh, and a little less rain tomorrow, please?"

Dang! She talks to Him like she knows Him.

Tawny turned around. "How's your supper?"

The mom glanced up, stopped chewing, swallowed.

"I have to say," she said. "This is the best pot roast ever. I don't even need a knife. You are *such* a good cook."

The woman tilted her head. *Will you smile now?*

Tawny went back to the kitchen. She checked her watch. *Won't be long.* She emptied the coffee pot into a to-go cup and pressed on a lid. She walked back onto the floor and over to their table.

"You all want dessert?" She hoped they'd say no.

The daughter shook her head. Tawny faced the mom.

She patted her stomach and groaned. "Sorry, no," she said. "I'm full as a tick on a bear's back."

One corner of Tawny's mouth went up. Ever so slightly. *There. I almost got you.*

Tawny gathered the empty side dish bowls and carried them back to the kitchen. The coleslaw bowl seemed to have been licked clean. That's when Tawny got the idea. *Maybe I can do it back.* She rested her elbows on the work surface and squinted at the mom through a space in the lattice.

Your eyes twinkle. Like the crystal thingy I have hanging on the rearview mirror in my Dodge. Randy always swore sooner or later the flashing would make someone wreck and they'd sue me. I don't care. It makes me happy and well, not a lot does these days.

The mom's eyes searched for and settled on Tawny. She grinned and the room seemed to shimmer. Tawny put her hand over her heart because it felt like it was coming out of her chest. She pretended to look down, but then she peered at the mom again, from under her bangs.

And I wish— Never mind.

Tawny totaled the check and laid it in front of the mother. "You can pay up at the register."

The mom's eyes narrowed, but not in a mad way. "Thank you."

Tawny gulped and inspected her shoes.

Thank you? For what? Did you hear me? A few minutes ago? When I looked at you and thought real hard?

She lifted her head slowly and found the mother's face. "For what?"

The woman lowered her mouth to the straw and sucked the dregs of her sweet tea. Her daughter cringed.

"For making us such an awesome supper."

Tawny glanced over her shoulder, toward Hugh and the grill. "I didn't—"

"I know," the mom said. "I'm just teasing."

Tawny watched the big, rainbow umbrella protect the mother and daughter as they made their way out to the Honda. She tried but couldn't hear their thoughts through the glass. When they got in the car, she moved to bus their table. The tip equaled the bill. Plus ten bucks.

Tawny peered out into the night. The Honda was there. Right outside the window. She saw the mother and daughter staring at her. She put her hand over her mouth. The mom's face shone. Sprinkles of light appeared on both sides of the window, even though it was night. And pouring the rain.

The mom and girl waved. Tawny rolled her fingers. Then her eyes filled and spilled over.

Odd

By Mary Lucille DeBerry

Because she wore fuchsia and lavender
taffeta blouses and long chambray skirts
above skimpy sandals, even in winter,
patrons of the library, particularly members
of "The Library Board" believed her to be
eccentric.

Her cigarette smoking outside on a bench,
while conversing with homeless men,
was a daily occurrence. Probably ... possibly,
board members conjectured, she "understood
them" better than any one else.

She corrected their misspelled words
when they wrote occasional letters
and, sometimes, she slipped them Sacagawea
coins for a gourmet cup of coffee.

She greeted everyone with a question
filled high with concern. She talked
about books and philosophy and reeled off
miles of appropriate quotations. There was not
an empty seat at her funeral.

Dog Days

By Barbara Smith

Crocker always reminds me and everyone else in town of Abraham Lincoln. He has that look about him—eyes that could look six ways at the same time, a jaw as long as a dime store nutcracker, and arms and legs that dangle, like one of those mountain dancing dolls. In short, Crocker Daly is one wart short of ugly.

He sounds dreadful, too. Squawks like a sick rooster or a pair of rusty brakes. Which reminds me of that time at the street fair when some Kentucky rube played snatches of a record for folks, real scratchy and skipping around, saying it was the only recording ever made of Honest Abe's voice. Said if folks would pay a quarter, he would allow them to step inside and hear the whole Gettysburg Address on the one side and the Emancipation Proclamation on the other. And you know, that jerk made him a bundle and a half of them quarters until some snake-spirited somebody, probably a Hatfield, persuaded the sheriff that recording devices were not readily available in 1865, and Abraham Lincoln never spoke the Emancipation Proclamation. He wrote it.

Anyhow, Crocker Daly looks like Lincoln and could have benefited just by dressing up and growing a beard and going from fair to fair with his hat held out.

But that was not what he had in mind.

See, he must of looked in the mirror one day and seen what the rest of us had been looking at for most of his growing-up years and all of his full-grown, and Crocker must of decided that if Abraham Whatever Lincoln, homely as that Illinois farm boy was, could get hisself called to Washington, D.C., U.S.A,. as the fourteenth president, then, his look-alike, old Crocker Daly, as look-alike as he indeed is, could also become a servant of the patriotic, peanut-headed public.

It took him twenty-seven months to gather up enough beer cans and pop bottles to pay for the printing of his first what-he-called broadside, which is the punchy little political term which translated means "piece of paper." He used all different colors of paper, my favorite of which was yellow, with all of the letters on all of those poster things being black. Thank God he did not put his picture on them. That would have done it for sure.

Now, the election Crocker was intent on winning was still more than a year away, but that boy is no dummy. The position he had in mind was a new one—nothing before ever like it either here nor in Estill County nor in Saltstone nor Maltby. This boy was set on carving out hisself a whole new kingdom.

And you know, he was aiming, if I did my share of things, to give me a slice of the pie. See, I am Crocker's second cousin once removed on my daddy's side, so my name is also Daly, as is that of this county on account of it is named after our granddaddy three or four times removed, who was one of them early settler types. That old buzzard, though probably at the time younger than Crocker or me is this minute, Crock being 28, me 26, cut him up and dug him out a couple hundred acres of squatter's land, and he built him a house of sorts and a mill there by the river, which is still here—the river, not the mill—and he also constructed him a ferry in the same general location, although on the water, and he staked him a couple of claims whether legitimately legal or not, whereby anybody coming or going across the river, which is the Wallowby, would have to use his ferry—or swim a mile—and pay him a nickel or dime depending on whether the guy had his wife and kids along, the latter being worth two cents each regardless of their age. Horses was six cents, cows four.

Anyhow, on account of that ferry/mill man, the town what grew up around was naturally called Daly's Mill, and that was some time or another—probably when the mill slid right into the river during a sizeable flood and hit the skids, as did the ferry—changed to Daly City. Should have been Dalyburg, emphasis on "burg." The whole county got to be Daly on account of that old geezer's brother, Crocker and me's great-great-something-uncle, donating the land for the courthouse, which has had a wet basement ever since the day it was born. Uncle Schuyler must have loved it. Mean old cuss as we hear tell.

So them handouts, pink and blue and yellow and green, showed up hanging from every telephone pole and pasted up in every store window, even the shut-down ones, and sticking out of every mailbox within fifty-seven miles. I ought to know—I done most of the pasting and sticking myself.

Following our wide distribution of the announcements, me doing most of the leg and footwork, Cousin Crocker begun working up public appearances, even with that squeaky little voice, the only one he happened to have. Anybody listening to Rooster Hour on WLOW of a weekend morning, few as those listeners was likely to be, heard Crocker from 5:30 to 6:30 a.m. spelling out what he called his platform and then answering calls from all them idiots, not me, of course, who feel compelled to listen to politics and police reports before the sun even comes up. Thinking about that, I wonder what all that ranting and raving does to milk production. I can just see old Elsie perking up her ears, so to speak, and rolling her big brown eyes when the announcer at WLOW opens up the airwaves and the microphone and says, so's he can go grab him a coffee and a Dunkin' Donut at Sheetz, which is right across the street from the station, which is upstairs of the NAPA store, "Good morning, all you bushy-tailed Dalyites, oh, a grand good morning to all of you fine people. This here is your good buddy and the sole owner of your favorite radio station, Ernie Koukulis, of WLOW, here in Daly City in the wild and wonderful state of West Virginia. We have a special guest with us this morning—again—and I don't want you to miss a single word of what this fine neighbor of ours has to say, so here he is in his lion's mane and peacock feathers, your friend and mine, Crocker J. Daly."

His middle name was originally Shill after his mama's daddy, but he changed that not only on account of what kids made of his name when we was all kids but also because, he tells it, he greatly admires the idea of Joshua and that battle at Jericho and the walls that was all knocked down. Thus he has become Crocker Joshua Daly.

Now, Crocker and me our whole lives has been writ off as the no-counts of the Daly clan on the basis of neither of us thinking school was the onliest or best way to learn what a fella has to know to be king or even just a second-level top dog like me. We did a lot of school-skipping, that's for certain, and had they caught us they could of put us away for life or almost in terms of the number of watermelons and apples and spare tires and such that we just happened upon now and again—as against murderers and sex fiends and that recent con artist whose name I cannot momentarily recall who stole the offering from St. Evan's Church because the day after Easter is also a holiday in the banks and the idiot priest (forgive me, Father, for I have sinned) left the offering plates right there on the altar in such plain sight as to tempt Mother Theresa her ownself.

Anyhow, that ungodly church robber and those sexists and murderers and such get off with a tweak on the cheek and a "sorry" from the judge while sad sacks like Crocker and me get sent up for life or more.

But we never did get caught, and here was Crocker and me running for this office. His platform on which I was also standing had just one plank in it, one good, admirable and honest purpose: "Daly's Goin' to the Dogs."

Now, you have to know that there is a legend, a custom, a what you call folkway where we come from and still abide. Dogs are sacred or near to it. That's why nobody who has any pride or sense raises sheep. Dogs, especially the wild type, like sheep, especially the lamb ones. You know what the Driver Education people always tell the kids—"Kill the deer, not yourself." Well, when it comes to dogs, that don't pertain.

Also, there is one other factor I got to bring to your remembrance. You ever watched that show *The Price Is Right*, which the women love because that Bob Barker was so god-awful handsome, even when he was in his dotage, and now that Drew Carey is just so god-awful funny or sexy or chummy or whatever? Well, old Bob Barker, before he ran off and retired, always used to sign off with what you surely can recall: "Control the pet population—have your pet splayed or neutraled." And he was right, even though Drew Carey has to all intents and purposes apparently decided it's not worth repeating.

The gerbil and parakeet population (splaying and neutralling probably wouldn't work on the latter but sure should on the former—they're like rats—a litter every minute) just keeps multiplying. Maybe they're even dividing into opposite parties that will in the foreseeable future attack each other, and then us humans, and take over the world, and then where would we be?

So here's how it is. Too many animals and too much unemployment, which is also growing almost as fast as cats and hamsters while at the same time people of taste like the rich and the famous in New York and Washington and Nashville cannot buy lamb even at Walmart or Kroger's, and Crocker and me are dead certain that were farmers and cattlemen to know sheep-raising as a viable commodity, they would line up like lemmings waiting for St. Patrick's appearance.

Any fool can see that the answer to this universal dilemma is to shoot the dogs, but that won't work. The first idiot who caught you zeroing in on a maverick mongrel would shoot you and turn the dog loose in your chicken coop.

So here comes Crocker, loaded for the proverbial bear—dog. He sets into making promises about improving the economy and raising the living standard, whatever that is, and putting Daly on the GPS, all by means of the dogs. And to illustrate his point and get a leaping start on the endeavor he is intending to establish, he bought him a slightly misused Toyota SUV, real cheap, and fitted it up, all but the front seat, to accommodate a passel of dogs. Away we then go.

First day following the distribution of handbills and the commencement of the radio program and Crocker's first speech-making, we rounded up seven in no time at all. Started around the back doors of the Burger King and the KFC where they have surrendered to Oprah and all those other fat-fighters and are going big-time with no longer being the fried chicken kings on the hill, and we rescued one little mutt from the side of the road where he had been dumped.

Took those seven creatures to Crocker's place and put them into the fences that Crocker had constructed and started in giving them shots and food and a whole bushel of soap and water, and by golly, we had us four winners and two also-rans and one pasture candidate. The former we figures as young and smart enough to learn a thing or two, and the also-rans would probably work into our program one way or another, and the decrepitist creature we'd just humor like everybody should any oldtimer.

That was the beginning, and I'm telling you, we was off and running, and so was the dogs. Crocker and me got us a couple of books from the library—first time we'd either one of us ever thought to darken that door—and we sent off for some free-bee stuff that we saw on TV, and we winged it when we had to, and you know, of the seventy-three pups we acquired in the next good-weather months, us building cages just as fast as we could, find the scrap lumber and abandoned fencing, and us begging and borrowing and, sure, stealing a little here and there, food and soap and all that stuff from every citizen of Daly County and beyond, we got us about forty-three good-working canines, and we put all but the senior canine citizens (about a dozen altogether) to immediate training and work, and now here's what we have and hire out:

    1. - Two teams of rescue dogs being used by the law enforcement and emergency crews of five counties

    2. - Nine therapy pups, the best-natured of the whole bunch, who are hired in ones or twos to go into hospitals and hospices and sick folks' homes to improve their morale and thus their general health

    3. - Seven narc dogs that the police of four counties support for obvious assignments and excursions

    4. - Nine trainees, still in the process of deciding how they're going to earn their—and our—livings.

We are also into breeding a few of the best of the bunch and are getting some pretty good offers for setting up rendevouses between our best studs and other people's bitches of pup-bearing condition. We are definitely, although lately, pro-life when it comes to dogs.

In the meantime, Crocker sure did get hisself elected dogcatcher, and he is now talking bigger next time, like maybe sheriff or assessor or county clerk, something which will make full use of his various talents and his increasing resources.

As for me, my ambitions have been stimulated as well. Our presently enscounced delegate to the state legislature is one of the corruptest ever to gaze on the golden dome of the capital building on the shores of the Kanawha River in the beautiful city of Charleston. It is my civic responsibility, I have come to believe, to displace that son-of-a-gun. I haven't broken a single law since we got us into the big-dog business, and I have become known as a community activist and am in the process of becoming church-oriented, and I have never beaten a single child or woman, and believe me, if Cousin Crocker, the all-time best Abraham Lincoln look-alike can do it, so can I. I am better looking than my dear old cousin, Crocker Daly.

Pee Wees' Playhouse

By Belinda Anderson

I blame Audubon for my trouble with the Eastern Phoebe. He affixed a silver wire to the leg of one of the rascals in 1840, and now the entire species thinks it's entitled to special privileges just because it may have been the first bird to wear an ankle bracelet.

The National Audubon Society, which provided that information, cheerfully states in its field guide that the bird calls out *phoe-be*, repeated many times with a distinctive short call note. I offer a few corrections: Incessant is a much more accurate term for "many times," and "piercing" pretty well describes the call, which sounded like *pee wee* to the ears of my mountain ancestors. The field guide also notes excitedly in italics that this bird, which dresses in neutral colors, *wags its tail*, as though this were some great accomplishment.

One morning, well before dawn, a pesky phoebe began bellowing outside my bedroom window. *Pee wee pee wee pee wee*. I stumbled into the bathroom, found some foam ear plugs and tried to finish my night's rest.

When I finally wandered outside the next morning into the pollen-laden air, I discovered that Ma and Pa already had filled out their change-of-address labels and begun slapping mud and moss atop one of my windows. This stumped me, as the window appeared to be installed flush against the side of the cabin.

But when I climbed the ladder that I had procured for patching woodpecker holes, I discovered that, indeed, the top of the window offered a small wedge of ledge. Never mind the fact that a luscious deciduous forest offered a plethora of housing opportunities mere yards away. I could see Pa pointing out how the eaves would protect the babies from the rain, how predators would never dream of hunting beneath the roof of a log cabin. "Oh, it's ideal," I could hear Ma chirp, quoting Sister in Eudora Welty's classic story, *Why I Live at the P.O.*

Armed with my free yardstick from the state fair, I scraped away the new housing development, descended the ladder, wrestled it into the outbuilding, and returned inside. The invasion having been averted, I dressed for hiking at the nearby Greenbrier State Forest—I love nature, just not attached to my own dwelling.

When I returned a few hours later, having admired a rare dwarf iris on one of the leaf-littered trails and listened to the call of crows who comprehend that trees make perfectly good nesting sites, I discovered that Ma and Pa had simply rebuilt on the site of the devastation. Once again, I hauled out the ladder and employed the yardstick to demolish the mossy mud foundation. Surely they'd be permanently discouraged.

Pee wee pee wee pee wee came my wake up call the next morning. This time, the message was for me: "Hee hee hee hee hee hee."

Once again, I discovered that the industrious Wees had been working hard. I dragged the ladder—and don't let anyone fool you that aluminum is all that light—to the construction site.

And then I had an epiphany. I returned to the house and brought out a dollar-store mirror, hanging it on the side of the house in what I hoped was the Wees' flight path. In theory, the pesky Wees would be tricked into thinking their mirror image was another bird flying in attack.

Returning home from my day's business, I found the mirror on the ground, but no evidence of a bird condominium. I've been pee wee free ever since.

Moral, courtesy of Walt Kelly's Pogo: *We have met the enemy and he is us.*

Bringing Home The Bacon

By Ginger Hamilton Caudill

First thing to do is feed that hog corn for about a month so's the meat won't be bitter. That softens the fat so's you can render it better. You kill him on the first full moon after the weather turns cold to stay, usually in November. Real early on slaughterin' day, you fill up a big old cast-iron caldron full of water and set it to boiling. The menfolk kill the hog by sticking his jugular vein right away. That's the one about three inches back from his jawbone.

When the bleedin' slows down, they drag him to the scaldin' place and dip him in the caldron. Then you roll him around to loosen the hair. It takes awhile to get it all off. You scrape, dip, scrape dip, keep on doin' that till most of the hair's off the hide. Don't leave him in the water for too long or the hair'll "set" instead of comin' loose.

Once you got him scraped clean, you find the hamstring on both of his hind legs. Then you take a gambling stick—that's just a stick sharpened at each end—and stick it behind the exposed leaders, or hamstring, and string the hog up on a sturdy pole. Stick the ends of the pole up between two forked supports or nearby trees so's he hangs free and clear of the ground. Then pour scaldin' water over him again to clean him off. Scrape him one more time for good measure – there's always hairs that get missed the first few times around. Now you can get started butcherin'.

First, you cut rings around his neck, just like a necklace. Then you twist his head off and set it aside. Later on you'll make souse from his head. Then you let him drain a little longer. Sometimes we put a little old pot underneath him to catch the blood; sometimes not. It ain't like it makes it any less messy.

You doin' okay there? You look a bit green around the gills. This ain't nothin', really. Been doin' it since time began. I know you like your bacon. Stand up straight so's you can pay attention.

Make a cut straight down starting at his crotch and run it all the way to the bottom. Pull that big container over here for me, will you? Now you make the second slice, going through the sack that holds—watch out there—his entrails. See how they tumble out and fall right into the tub, pretty as you please? Then you cut 'em off at the top, pull the skin up and tie 'em off up here. Next cut 'em off at the bottom and do the same thing. That keeps the offal inside. We'll clean up the intestines later on when we make our chitterlings, but we need to get him fixed up first.

This part's simple here. You just cut each organ loose one at a time and let it drain. Then wash 'em and set 'em in cold water to soak while you finish the cuttin'. Just be careful when you go to slicing the stomach and small bowel off of the entrails; you don't want to nick 'em or else you'll have a stink you wouldn't believe. Bring a tear to your eye, it would.

Get a sausage pot a-goin' to put the leaner meat into, and a ren-derin' pot for fat trimmings. We won't be renderin' today; that'll come tomorrow. Too much work in one day can kill a body, you know it? You cut out this here leaf lard—that's the fat that clings around his entrails—and toss it in the renderin' pot. Then slice him straight down the center of his back, right into the backbone. Now you can either take him down yourself to do the rest of the cutting, or call somebody to help. First time I tried it alone, my hands were so slicky I liked to never got him situated. Set him on his back, on a board or cutting table. Take an axe and chop straight down on both sides of his backbone and lift it right out. The meat will fall into two hunks.

Take out the tenderloins. See 'em there on either side of what's left? Right beneath them is your fatback. You can cook that right by itself, makes good eatin'. Remove the ribcage by cuttin' between the outside of his ribs and the inside of the middlin' meat. Each section oughta come out in one piece.

Feel around and find his joints there. They feel just like a person's joints do. Cut the shoulders and hams off and set them on some-thing clean along with the tenderloins, like a tarp or another table.

Now what you got left is the side meat. Some folks call it the mid-dlin'. This here thick section of meat on each side is your country bacon, once it's cured and smoked. Just slice the bacon off of the side meat, cuttin' the same direction as the ribs run. Some folks make "streak'a'lean" out of the bacon. It ain't smoked, just salt-cured. I prefer bacon to streak'a'lean, don't you?

Leave the rest of it to the menfolk. They'll take those ribs and put `em on a choppin' block and cut the sections into two-inch-wide strips. Later on, we'll can those along with the backbone. They'll cut it apart at each section—makes it easier to can.

Ferdy over there'll trim up the hams, shoulder, and side meat. The part he trims off will go right into the rendering or sausage pots. What don't go into the pots gets salted right away so's the flies don't blow it. Like I told you, the backbones and ribs'll get canned. We'll cook those tenderloins and the other organs—heart, lungs, liver, kidneys, plus his head—right now. Sausage will be ground up and canned this afternoon. We can leave these fat scraps till tomorrow when we cut `em up and render the lard.

Tomorrow, I'll teach you how we render the scraps and cure the bacon. Right now I think you need a rest. You look a bit green. Wash your hands real good and we'll go have lunch.

Canning Beans

By Frances Lucretia Van Scoy

Just outside Fairmont, West Virginia, stands a covered bridge. The bridge is older than the state of West Virginia but younger than most of the local families' ancestors. When the bridge was about ten years old, Jones's raiders tried to burn it down, but some local people stopped them. They lied and told the invaders that they and the bridge were loyal to the Confederacy, so the soldiers marched through the bridge and left it standing.

After the war, a man built a house on a nearby rise with a sweeping view of the covered bridge, the stream it spans, the curving country road, and the mountains that surround the valley. Time passed and generation after generation of his family lived in that house. Often, on summer evenings after all the work was done, they would sit on the front porch talking to each other, listening to bob whites in early summer or crickets in late summer, and looking at the covered bridge until it was so dark that the bridge could scarcely be seen. The covered bridge was always there and always part of the family.

But a few generations ago the covered bridge lost its place as favorite special family member to an exceptionally large tree that stood in the front yard. This tree was so near the house that some branches were reachable from the windows of one upstairs bedroom.

"Catalpa" is the name most people use for trees like this one, but the family called theirs a "stogie" tree. When the father was a young man, he had worked in Wheeling at a cigar factory. People called cigars of one kind made at the factory "stogies." Some said the name "stogie" was short for "Conestoga wagon," the kind of covered wagon used by travelers crossing Pennsylvania and traveling through Wheeling in the pioneer days of the 19th century.

Supposedly, the shape of the large cigar reminded some of the earlier cigar workers of the cloth cover on a Conestoga wagon. And the shape of the stogie cigar resembled the shape of the long brown seed pods of the catalpa tree, so local people started calling catalpa trees "stogie" trees.

Now, some people don't like catalpas. They say they're "dirty" trees because of the long seed pods they shed. But for the children of this family the seed pods were part of what made the tree so special. They claimed as their own their mother's cracked canning jars and damaged metal rims and used sealing lids. Then they pretended to "can beans" as they stuffed catalpa seed pods into the jars.

From sunrise to sunset the children could be found around the tree—climbing it, swinging on a tire swing, sitting on a branch, or leaning against the trunk while reading a book. In the summer a blanket thrown over the lowest branch made a fine tent. Except on the coldest days of winter the children seemed to spend more time in or near the tree than in the house. The neighbors often said the catalpa tree raised those children.

Every year the family reunion gathered in the yard of the old house, with several flat bed farm wagons functioning as serving tables. The grandparents, the aunts and uncles, and the cousins all came for the day, and the older folk sat in chairs under the tree to enjoy its shade.

Early one summer one of the boys tried to use the tree to help him run away from home. He was angry at his parents for some reason now long forgotten. That evening he sneaked some food from the supper table into his pants pocket he had lined with wax paper. After the children were all sent to bed, he wrapped the food in the wax paper and slipped it into the middle of a bundle of clothes he had prepared earlier in the day. His parents were still downstairs when he went into their bedroom, opened the window, and reached for the nearest branch of the catalpa. He grabbed the branch and swung out the window. The branch bent more than he had expected, and the bundle of clothes and food under his arm began to slip. As he reached for the bundle with one hand, his other hand lost its grip on the tree, and he fell with a loud crash. His parents heard the noise and rushed outside. He had broken his leg. At first he was angry at the tree for causing him to fall. But as he spent the remaining months of summer in the shade of the catalpa waiting for his leg to heal, he realized that in a way he felt grateful to the tree for keeping him from the dangers of life on the road.

When the oldest daughter became engaged, she decided to hold her wedding reception in the front yard. The family borrowed folding tables and chairs from their church and set up the table for the wedding party right next to the tree. At the reception, after the best man had toasted the couple with ginger ale and orange sherbet punch, one of the bride's brothers stood up and said that the bride's good friend, Stogie, had asked him to read a pair of toasts.

"Carl, congratulations on persuading Avis to accept your proposal of marriage.

Treat her well, or you'll have to deal with me."

"Avis, I'll miss you terribly. In fact I might turn into a weeping willow as I cry because of missing you. But promise me that you'll bring your future children to visit me often."

When the oldest son went off to war, the younger children tied yellow ribbons to the branches of the tree, and when he was discharged from the army his "welcome home" party was held in the tree's shade.

But one year just before Thanksgiving the father had a heart attack. Everyone said the father was too young to have a heart attack, but nonetheless it happened. He had to quit his job in the coal mine, but he thought he could keep up with the farm chores with the help of his sons.

At Christmas a cousin came back home from Akron for a visit. He had moved to Akron twenty years earlier and worked in a tire factory. He told the father that the tire plant always needed new workers and that some of the jobs weren't demanding physically. The father wasn't interested. He said he was really looking forward to working in the fields come spring.

When spring came, the father realized that he couldn't keep up with the farm chores, even with the help of his sons. The family sold their two milk cows and their small flock of chickens to a neighbor, put their farm up for sale, and prepared to move to Akron so the father could work at the tire factory.

The children were sad to leave the only home they had ever known and the covered bridge, but they were especially sad to leave Stogie.

In late fall, as they were moving out of the house, the man who had bought the house started moving in. One family member said it was sad to leave the catalpa tree. The new owner quickly said that the tree was one of the reasons he had bought the house! Everyone felt better after that.

Life in Akron was hard. Instead of living in a two story farm house with a big front yard and fields and a woodlot to explore, they lived in an apartment. Milk now came from the store in a bottle and was always cold, not warm as it came fresh from the cow. And milk was homogenized. It didn't separate into a thick layer of rich cream floating above the milk. Cottage cheese came in a carton from the store, because mother no longer made it on the back of a wood-fired stove. When spring came, they had no place to raise a garden, and they knew there would be nothing for the mother and the girls to can in the fall. The apartment was much smaller than their old house. So most rooms had boxes not yet unpacked because there was no place to put anything.

Then in May a phone call came. Grandmother had died. The family piled into their old station wagon and went back to West Virginia for the funeral.

After the funeral, the father decided to take a side trip before heading back to Akron and drove past their old house. The family was full of anticipation as they turned onto the familiar gravel road. Their excitement grew as they went around the last curve and saw the covered bridge. But their excitement turned to dismay when they saw in their beautiful big catalpa tree was a jagged stump! Father stopped the car, and everyone looked in silence. There in the front yard sat the man who had bought the house. He was whistling as he carved a piece of wood. On one side of him were chunks of the catalpa tree. On the other side was a table with ugly junk: miniature outhouses, poorly shaped farm animals, and distorted figures of "hillbillies," all carved from the catalpa.

The children started to cry. A bolder child got out of the car, approached the man and said, "I thought one reason you bought our house was the tree."

"I did," he said. "I make things to sell at flea markets, and that tree was so big I knew I could make lots of money from it."

It was a doubly sad ride back to Akron as the family mourned the loss of both the grandmother and the catalpa tree. Over the next few days if anyone mentioned the tree or the old house the children burst into tears. The younger children drew pictures of the house and the tree. The older children were sad and didn't say much.

Then in the fall the parents bought a house in a small town near Akron. The house had many rooms and a yard to play in and room for a garden.

After this second move, it was fun unpacking the boxes from the farm. There were clothes and toys they had forgotten about. Most of the clothes were now too small for their previous wearers, but these were passed down to a younger child. To everyone's surprise, one box was full of cracked canning jars, each stuffed full of seed pods from their old catalpa tree!

At Christmas when the oldest children came home with their own young children to the new house, they were each given a canning jar full of catalpa seeds. And come spring the younger children planted two catalpa seeds in the yard of their new house, and the grown-up children did the same at their houses.

Years went by, and the new trees grew a foot or two each year. Sometimes there were sad good-byes as families moved to new houses. They hugged the catalpas they were leaving behind, but moved the jars of remaining catalpa seeds to new houses, and once again planted seeds in new yards.

Years later, when the grandchildren had children of their own, every family had at least one large catalpa in their yard. The youngest generation spent long summer days with their own special catalpa trees, while their parents and grandparents watched and smiled.

The Song

By Jason Roth

As the fog lifts over the hollow
Life comes into view
Phantasmagorical blobs transform themselves
Into trees of golden hue.
The creek runs 'round the bend
babbling as it rolls over gravel beds.
A breeze blows through the branches
Rustling leaves like nodding heads.
Stop and listen just a moment
As the sun warms the earthly fountain
The frogs croaking, the dove mourning
And hear the song of the mountain.

Calling Me Home

By Christine Roth

The mountains are within me,
calling me home when I am far away.
An ache resounds and echoes when I hear that West Virginia twang,
making my need all the more fierce.

I remember the mountains, the sight of them before me.
Foggy mornings, mist rolling up from the ground,
surrounding the mountaintops like bridal veils.
Then it creeps back down, covering the roads,
misting over the Kanawha River.

And all I can say is "Take me home please. Take me back to my mountains."
I am being called home.

Let me see the mountains along the interstate towards Elkins,
the lights of Charleston from on top of Bridge Road,
and the murals along the walls of Pt. Pleasant as the Mothman looks on.
I want to smell wood smoke, to hear the cheer "Let's Go Mountaineers!!"

Please take me back,
she is calling me there.
West Virginia is my mountain mama
and she is calling me back there.

On Hearing Bill Withers
in the Ninth Grade

By Marion R. Kee

thank you God he got out and then came back to us
on the radio we heard him and it was the voice of home
we knew it like the mountains up there always from the start
it was the voice that cradled us
it is the voice will sing us to our graves
powerful, big as rivers,
rick like honey on biscuits—
we knew his voice
and Lord, we knew he made it out.

We could hear he was a genius
And a black man
From the coal mining country
Oh Lord we knew
He got out, Lord, we knew he made it out.

He made it big somewhere out there in L.A.
But we knew he paid the price, he don't come home
We knew he paid the price, he said, 'bout getting' used
But we heard him say it from L.A.
Lord, we knew he made it out.

Some said he came from Cabin Creek,
Some said Alum Creek, said Coal River,
Some said Beckley but they didn't know
They was right 'bout that—
They was all kind of rumor 'bout him they all said
Lord, he was a black man and a genius from the coal country
And Lord, he made it out,
                    He made it, out there in L.A.

.

The Forgetting

By Mathilde Hall

We don't know when it started.
It slowly snuck up, little by little.

First, she got lost at the Grand Central Mall.
Got turned around, somehow. Lost her way.
We laughed. Thought it was funny. No big deal.

Then she forgot to wear a bra.
Once again, we laughed,
until, in embarrassment, she cried.

Next, she went to the mailbox,
make-up applied to perfection, hair coiffed artfully,
wearing only her periwinkle, see-through nighty.
That seemed peculiar, even to us.

She was strong. Could briskly walk
two miles without getting out of breath.
Then, suddenly, her knees would buckle,
and without warning, she'd fall to the ground.

Most mornings, her husband hung out her soiled
satin sheets to dry. When she was aware,
she would stare toward the clothesline and wail.

She began to eat with her fingers, dripping gravy
and yellow juices on her blouse.
From then on, it was simple clothes for her,
like T-shirts and sweats, with Depends worn underneath.

She sat in her favorite chair most days
and watched television, constantly standing up

and sitting back down like a slowly worked yoyo.

When she started to fall daily, once even getting herself wedged between the tub and the commode, her husband couldn't do it anymore. He put her into a home.

That's when she forgot to eat. Then she forgot to breathe.

Holding Memories

By Beverly Bisbee

A sliver of soap brings a memory. Your back, as I washed its soft skin, was as lovely as the day you were born, and I told you so. Your answer, humbly spoken, was that your mother always told you the same thing. The soap remains in the tray, and I use it sparingly, fearing that when it disappears, I may forget the mornings when I bathed you.

Though our guests may choose to sit in your chair, the one where crossword puzzles were completed or put aside, they never fill the seat with the same possessiveness. It belongs to you even now. Crumbs and tissues, stuffed deep in the folds, continue to appear even after the vacuum cleaner has explored the corners. The cats, though they may claw the back, find themselves on its cushion napping, as if they remain on your lap.

Your sisters came and tried on garments that continue to hold your scent. The blouses that once adorned your bosom found the breasts of your siblings. Their feet slipped into your many high-heeled shoes, but their walk was not yours. Yet, I observed this and thought that you would have preferred this dispersing, this fashion show of years, and their selections for new ownership. They told stories of your meticulousness, your finding just the right dress in the best of stores, and the confidence you carried when wearing these clothes. They displayed sisterly love for the example you set. I thought there would be more laughter, more humor, but there was a tone of sweet respect, a quiet in the delight of holding what once held you.

The door to your room is closed, but I go in to breathe your air and just remember. Instead of thinking about illness and a hospital bed, I wish I could dwell on years ago when you carried a teakettle and watered the plants in that long flower box that bordered our front porch. Daddy's spring ritual of bringing in rich soil from the woods and taking you to the greenhouses, as we tagged along, taught us to learn the fragrances of both forest and floral, and promoted similar scenes we have repeated with our own families. The front porch flower box was complete when you stood next to it, your hands sprucing up the blooms. When I cut some of your driveway zinnias and sold them door-to-door, you explained that a growing flower is much more valuable than a cut one. You told me that I had to donate the $1.89 to the March of Dimes; your lesson, delivered with kindness, had layers of meaning and a residual effect.

I wish I could revisit that old house where you waited for us to come home from school, especially the days when opened windows aired out the rooms and the curtains waved us in. The smell of bleach announced all germs had been conquered. You were indeed particular about caring for our home and for us. Your hands would pull the washed clothes through the wringer, and you would caution me never to let my fingers get caught between the horizontal cylinders. You showed me how to hang clothes on the line correctly, and the smell of those sun-dried garments made carrying them into the house an easy task.

I never heard you complain, but when you would compare my hands with yours and note the thirty-year difference, I saw how the hard work had aged them. Yet, you were proud as you polished your nails, and humored as I sat beside you playing manicurist.

I know there is an embroidered quilt in a box somewhere that your hands never finished, and I know there is a box of my father's love letters tied with a pink ribbon for me to read. When I write my signature, I know it resembles yours, and I know I carry your name. When I think of words not spoken, I know that there wasn't a need.

When grieving and remembering are blended, my mind and emotions struggle to coexist. Like the sliver of your soap that I am treasuring, I want to hold on to you.

Broken Chain

By Patricia Hopper Patteson

No one was more surprised than I was to learn my mother had been adopted—fostered out when she was born. It was a closely guarded secret until my sister Colette decided to become Mormon and probe into our family background. She shared the strange story with me while sitting on a bench in Memorial Gardens one day.

These are not gardens in the usual sense; there is no grass, flowers, or trees. Ponds with underwater vegetation are surrounded by a maze of concrete walks and enclosed by a stone wall that separates them from Upper O'Connell Street. Tourists seldom come here. It's a sanctuary known mostly to Dubliners who seek a place to rest, eat lunch, or like us, sit and talk.

On that day, Colette opened her leather bag and took out a large brown envelope. She held it on her lap but didn't open it.

"I have something to tell you," she said.

"What?" I asked.

"It's about Mam." She drew a deep breath. "Mam's name is not Doyle, it's Kinneavy. She was—fostered out."

I stared at her is disbelief. "What do you mean—fostered out?"

"She's not a Doyle."

"How do you know that?"

"I found out accidentally."

"Did Mam tell you?"

"No. I did a genealogy of the family. Dad's side was pretty straightforward but when I searched Mam's birth record under Doyle, I found nothing. I told Mam and she brushed me off saying it was probably lost or something. I was insistent and she finally relented, told me Doyle wasn't her real name, that the Doyles were her foster family. That's when things got bizarre. I found her birth certificate under Kinneavy; the mother was named, but the father was unknown. I traced Mam's mother to Connemara. The records I found are in here."

Colette patted the envelope and frowned. "I went over to Con-

79

nemara and talked to some Kinneavys, but you know how close-mouthed people are in the West when strangers ask questions, especially about family."

I sat bewildered, trying to make sense of what my sister was saying.

"I tried to piece together what happened," Colette continued. "Mam's mother Bridget, Elizabeth Kinneavy, went into domestic service for a landowner in a house called Ebor Hall when she was old enough. It was the only employment available to girls in that part of Connemara in those days. After Bridget went to work there, the son became infatuated with her and before long she found herself pregnant.

"People viewed pregnancy differently back in the 1920's. It meant shame, and in Bridget's case, a possible threat to the landlord's family. So she was paid off, £300, a fortune, enough to get her to Dublin and sustain her for a long time."

Colette paused and I asked, "Is she still alive?"

"Yes." Colette motioned for me to let her finish.

"While Bridget lived in Dublin, she became acquainted with the Doyles. She told them she planned to give up her baby to foster care. After Mam was born, the Doyles offered to take her as their own. Soon after that Bridget emigrated to America. She lives in Pennsylvania, not far from where you are in West Virginia."

Colette handed me the brown envelope. I stared at it, wanting to throw it into the depths of the ponds just feet away, yet held spellbound by its contents. In one quick swoop my sister had unraveled our family core. She had undone our link to a past that was securely founded and had thrown us into the path of some unknown origin.

With her secret finally out in the open, my mother began to talk about her fosterage. It was a blemish that had plagued her all her life, one she kept hidden because of the questions it presented and the answers certainly too painful to bear.

After that day in Memorial Gardens, the question of parentage hung in the air, muted by the distance that separated me from Ireland and my sister. At one point I decided to contact the woman who was thought to be our grandmother. During my phone conversation with her son Tom, I learned she'd had a slight stroke, but he invited me to visit her at his home in Pennsylvania anyway.

I arrived at the appointed time and was welcomed by the woman and her son. As we talked I stayed alert, receptive to everything about her, looks, feelings, thoughts, words. I ached to know if she was family, I wanted to feel it intuitively. But my instincts were clouded. I found that I had conjured up her image in my mind; I'd imagined she would look like my mother only older, same face, smile, hazel eyes, and that image crept between the woman and me.

I searched the woman's face for familiarity, but there was little resemblance, only the occasional facial expression and dark hair still visible through gray. She wore a plain dress, heavy black shoes and was tall, possibly taller than my mother. Her words came slow, lazy, with a trace of Irish accent.

Neither she nor her son asked how I was knowledgeable about the Kinneavys. They accepted that I was related; the question "to whom" was never asked. Together we looked through a book my sister had given me about Lough Corrib that was filled with old photos of the Kinneavy family, of places known to the woman when she was a young girl. She talked about people she knew, their lives, their homes, their offspring. I strained for information that might cement my connection to this woman, this place. I sifted through words for clues, only to find more questions than answers.

By the end of the visit, I had not asked the crucial question—was Bridget Kinneavy my grandmother? When I thanked the older woman for the visit, her son handed me his business card. I put it in my wallet for safekeeping where it still sits.

Colette had tried from time to time to fit the pieces of the puzzle together. In 1994, years after she had told me about my mother's fosterage, she was ready to try again. I was hardly over jet lag on my visit home that year when Colette suggested we go to Connemara. I could see she had been waiting for this from the moment I had gotten off the plane.

A couple of days later we set out on the drive from Dublin to Galway which takes about three hours and stretches coast to coast across the plains of Ireland. Nearing the West, pastures gradually gave way to rugged countryside and town names began to appear in Irish; this is the Gealtacht region where the Irish is spoken. Galway, now the booming metropolis of the West, sits at the edge of the Atlantic. Here the modern and traditional flourish side by side, with a sprinkle of Mediterranean.

From Galway we turned onto the road north that winds along the west bank of Lough Corrib, the second largest fresh-water lake in Ireland. Once past the small town of Oughterard mountains hug the skyline as the road climbs into rugged terrain, strewn with sheep and occasional patches of purple heather. Dooras, the only peninsula on the lake, is on the northwest side, and here we stopped. It was among a smattering of houses along a narrow stretch of road jutting into Lough Corrib that Bridget Kinneavy had grown up. We parked the car and strolled down the deserted road, Colette probing her memory for the house that might have been the one where our grandmother had spent her youth. We sat on a low wall and watched the sun begin to fall behind the mountains. On the lake fishermen sat calmly in slow moving boats patiently waiting to hook a fish.

It was easy to imagine Bridget coming to this quiet place to think about her lover. She would have been religiously naïve knowing only that men and women "coupled" after marriage, an intimacy held in the conclaves of married women and talked about in hushed whispers. Chastity would have been preached with premarital sex referred to obliquely as "any impure thought or deed." Perhaps it was here she had said her goodbyes, disillusioned, shamed, pregnant, and condemned to exile.

We passed through the village of Cornamona that sits close to the Dooras peninsula, nothing more than some shops, pubs, a church, a school, and a post office. The road wound upward toward our accommodation, Island View, a long bungalow turned bed and breakfast. It sat snugly on a mountainside, overlooking fields tied together by low rock walls and joined in locked tandem until they disappeared out of sight at the edge of Lough Corrib.

The owner of Island View was Mary Morrin, formerly Mary Kinneavy. She opened the door to us, a woman in her mid-thirties, petite, her short hair streaked blond. She smiled from clear blue eyes set in a serene face with a creamy complexion. In a soft-spoken voice she directed us to our rooms explaining where everything was. Then excusing herself she disappeared into another part of the house.

The following morning we ate breakfast in the dining room with a breathtaking view of the lake and its islands. It was a bright summer's morning, and we decided to travel the few miles to Cong, a village at the most northern point of the Corrib, that still boasts (over fifty years later) the filming of that classic movie *The Quiet Man*.

Ashford Castle stands at the edge of the village surrounded by gardens, a black stone structure riveted against the sky. From these grounds on the banks of Lough Corrib, boats shuttle tourists to Inchagoill (Island of the Stranger) the largest island on the Corrib and once home to the Kinneavys.

We passed through stone arches with high towers on either side, across the wooden bridge to the inlet where a boat was moored that would take us to Inchagoill. With its passengers safely on board, the boat pushed off onto what seemed like a freshly painted canvas—blue sky, sparkling clear water, Ashford castle dominating the background. Blooming flowers and neat lawns spread to the lake dotted with islands, and mountains rose in the foreground in various shades of green.

A guide met us at Inchagoill and took us ashore. We toured the ruins of two ancient churches, Teampall Phádraig, dating to the fifth century, and Teampall na Naomh, twelfth century. We were shown a slim, ancient gravestone with Roman script that is said to mark the grave of St. Patrick's nephew, Lugna.

Tall trees towered close and pathways led to unknown parts of the island. The guide, afraid of losing patrons kept the group together, leaving no time for exploration. It was a large island, one hundred thirty three acres, eighty of it tillable and once occupied by several families. All that was left of that existence was the house and steam boiler that once belonged to Martin Kinneavy, a boat builder on the island.

"Imagine the isolation here," Colette said. "It has a Robinson Crusoe feeling. For centuries these were island people, before they moved inland. They fished, farmed, built houses, and traveled in boats. Just think, this is where it all began."

On our return voyage we approached our navigator, John, a stout man with gray hair and thick eyebrows. We were told in Cong that he knew the area well.

"You're from around here?" I ventured.

"Been here all my life," he replied.

"Have you ever heard of Ebor Hall?"

He gave me a curious look. "Tis on the road to Cornamona, about three miles outside Cong. Ye can't miss it, 'tis high on the hill to your right. Ye'll see the wall first."

"Do you know anything about the families that lived there?"

"It has a long history, seen quite a few owners down through the years. The most famous was Mountmorris, but the house has changed hands several times since then." John maneuvered the boat into the dock making it difficult to talk as people moved forward to debark. With the last passenger gone we picked up the conversation. "The reason we're inquiring," I said, "is that we believe we're related to one of the owners of the house."

"Thanks be to God," John exclaimed, looking from my sister to me. "Tis detectives I thought the pair of ye were." He paused. "Lord Mountmorris was murdered and the house is said to be haunted after that. It sat idle for a period of time before it was taken over again."

"Do you know when that was?" Colette asked.

"Can't be sure. Late eighteen hundreds, maybe."

"Do you know who the new owners were?" she prodded. "Were they related to Mountmorris?"

"The name was Boyd, a physician he was." John said. "That's who took over the house. I've no idea what year t'was."

John didn't know any more than what he'd told us and as we left he said, "Good luck girls, I'll pray that ye find what yer looking for."

It rained that night. We could hear it beating against the bedroom window. The sky was overcast when we sat down to breakfast next morning. The lake was bleak, the water dark, the mountains even darker. Long grass swayed in the wind. On the road to Cornamona and Dooras we found the wall that enclosed Ebor Hall. Trees hovered above, hiding the house from curious eyes. Workers were repairing the gatehouse at the entrance of the drive and we asked permission to go up to the house.

A man in charge said he didn't see any harm in us taking a look since the owners were away. We walked up the long drive, past well-kept lawns to where the house stood with a commanding view of the land and the Corrib. The large square structure several stories high dominated the scene. A feeling of spaciousness prevailed: wide lawns, trees set back away from the house, stucco walls freshly painted white, heavy Georgian front door, long windows with wide sills, chimneys that peeked above the roof, smokeless.

Wide concrete steps led to the front door, to windows where we peered inside at large rooms. Colette voiced my desire. "If only we could go inside," she said. We walked around the house inspecting it. There was quiet all around, except for the wind whining through the treetops. If Mountmorris claimed this home, his ghost was quiet, out of reach on this gloomy day.

It began to rain lightly and we decided to go into Clonbur for lunch. This we had in a small pub. We feasted quietly on chicken, carrots, potatoes covered with gravy, and thick slices of soda bread. We listened to the locals speak Gaelic in a dialect that was hard to follow, although my sister's ear is keener than mine.

That evening when the rain diminished we walked along the wet, misty banks of the Corrib, the air heavily scented. It was easy to see how traditional ways prevailed here. Remnants of ancient tribes and early Christians are scattered throughout the countryside along with reminders of mythological times. On close by Moytura, legend has it that the Tuatha De Danann defeated the Fir Bolg in a major battle. According to folklore, the battle fought between these two races was done with the help of druids and magicians. To mark the momentous occasion, the area is fraught with long-ago monuments, stone circles and cairns that give claim to these legendary notions. As the water slapped against the banks of the Corrib in the calm misty evening, it was easy to imagine images and hear voices of that long-ago past.

The next morning we dawdled before our departure from Island View hoping to speak to Mary. Colette was first to find her alone and was in the middle of telling our story to a surprised hostess when I found them. "I'm afraid I can't help much," Mary was saying. "I don't know that side of the family well; there was a split a long time ago."

"A fight between two brothers and they never spoke to each other afterwards," Colette said.

"Yes," Mary acknowledged. "It caused a rift. I hardly know the Dooras Kinneavys. But there is talk of getting everyone together for a reunion. You're welcome to come if you'd like. People here have long memories and some of the older ones might know what happened. You could talk to them."

It was well into the afternoon when we said goodbye to Mary along with a promise to stay in touch. We left on the road along the east coast of the Corrib, through the small villages of Headford and Carrandulla, the lake visible along the way. As we drew closer to the Galway road, the lake faded slowly out of sight and was replaced by bogland and stacks of turf drying in fields.

We had hoped to return from the West knowing more about our mother's origin and to assuage her childhood fears. Although we didn't find tangible evidence that tied us to the Corrib, we found a sense of belonging there: a sense of being that serves as an antidote against difficult days; a place to reflect inward during times filled with anxiety and haste. Possibly all we accomplished was to embellish the mystery that begot our ancestry, a fate destined to become mythicized like the many ancient stories that abound in Ireland.

Our grandparents who could've told all had already passed away. With time marching on, the answers of what happened to Bridget

Kinneavy has become more and more difficult to resurrect, a truth lost in time. The past may never be fully uncovered, but I found a sense of connectedness, combined with elusive longing that will draw me back time after time to the Corrib.

The Green Children

By Susan Sheppard

Led with delight they thus beguile the way,
Untill blustering storme is overblown;
When weening to return, whence they did stray,
They cannot finde that path, which first was showne,
But to wander to and fro in ways unknown.
~Edmund Spenser—The Faerie Queene

They left a forest of beautiful gloom
Leaving their brood of green,

Abandoned a cave made of fern
To follow the invisible horses

Of human longing

Where the sky broke open
To the reveal the furnaces of heaven.

It was an infatuation with the sound
Of tiny bells that drew them out,

Wishing only to join the spirits of the meadow
With green lamps hitched to their tails.

Still the sun blistered their eyes, stunned
Them into forgetting their green fractured world.

Among the hemlocks and the yew,
In the black and mortal forest
Came an indelicate rising of ghosts.

Even so there was a leafy

Dampness to their skins,
A smell of sod where owls
With the eyes of cats lifted from the limbs.

Clasping hands like braided flowers,
They vanished to join the weird
Elixirs of the moon.

Ivy and Fern, with names divine,
How they died in the grass like dew.

The Climb

By Lynne Schwartz-Barker

The dark-haired, dark-eyed boy climbed the slicky slide's worn silver ladder. He examined each step for potential danger while tightly grasping the handrails. At the top, he carefully swung his legs forward before gliding down the metal chute.

Julia, a tall 35 year-old blonde, anxiously watched from a rough wooden bench, wondering what he was thinking. It was a cool, cloud covered morning in these high mountains and she pulled the blue wool sweater closely around her. Martin, the little boy, in a thin shirt and shorts, showed no sign of discomfort or emotion: no smile, no giggle, no flash of fear, just intense concentration. At the bottom of the slide, he didn't pause or glance in her direction on his way to the ladder for the next eight step ascent.

Climb, sit, slide. Climb, sit, slide. How many times had he done the same routine in the hour they'd been there? *Like a playground robot*, she thought. *If I timed him, I'll bet each trip would be the same.*

It's not what she expected from a boy. She'd grown up in a rural area with three older brothers and often engaged in their rough and tumble high jinks, punching and wrestling, playing jokes on each other. This boy, *her boy* she kept reminding herself, wasn't like that. He was cautious, remote, unreachable. A dozen other children played on the swings and seesaws and he didn't interact with them. Not when a bigger boy shoved him out of the way to be first up the slide, not when two girls made faces and waggled tongues at him. *So serious. So shy. Of course, he doesn't know any of them.*

She too felt self-conscious, a stranger in this strange land of small dark people who spoke a language she couldn't understand. Three thousand miles from home, she longed for the warmth and support of her husband John and her family in the West Virginia hills.

A photo, a paragraph, and a prayer had brought her to this playground. The first two spilled out of an envelope with a letter from an adoption agency. "Martin is a five year old boy, slightly behind in development, who needs a family to love him." The photo

91

showed a beautiful child with a shy hint of a smile. He looked younger, small for his age, with heavy eyelids that slanted upwards at the corners.

"He sure doesn't look like our family," her blue-eyed husband John said, with a chuckle. "And what does slightly behind in development mean?" Julia worried about this too. Would the boy be able to keep up in school or was he already forever scarred at five years old? She called the agency to inquire, but no one could answer her questions. It was a stock phrase for older children, waiting to be adopted.

The prayer spilled out of her heart, asking for guidance. Was this their child, the one they'd waited so many years for? How could they know with only a photo and a paragraph? Julia had stared at that photo over and over again, brushing Martin's face with her fingertips, searching for a clue. It haunted and broke her heart—so much sadness in that boy's smile, so much longing. Was he aching for a family, the way she ached for a child? Her husband felt that longing too, so she wrote, "Yes, we'll take him" to the agency.

From the playground, she gazed out to the sharply peaked mountains, so like the breasts of a young woman. Her mountains, the ones back home, were older, smoother, rounder, more the bosom of a comforting mother. Could this boy be happy in and comforted by them too? Would he climb the hills with his new family, quietly watching deer saunter by the fern-rich hollow they lived in? Would he pick a sack full of black walnuts in autumn with John or hunt for crawdads in the creek?

There was no autumn here, only dry and rainy seasons. There was no winter, no snow. Would Martin find delight in the fluffy white flakes? Catch them on his tongue? Lie down in them to make snow angels? Julia studied the boy's expressionless face. *Does he even know what delight is? Has he ever known? Am I capable of teaching him?*

Julia had ached for a child for almost ten years and now she'd finally have one. Years of infertility, years of miscarriages, and a failed attempt at adoption with a young woman who had broken Julia's heart when she decided to keep her baby. She was propelled forward by a single-minded goal—to be what so many millions of women were so easily, a mom.

At home she'd imagined meeting Martin. Julia had the romantic notion it would be mutual love at first sight. The sweet little boy would rush into his new parents' arms. He would excitedly try on the sweaters and pants she'd lovingly bought for him, wrestle and giggle with John and they would begin to form a family. The reality was quite different. As adoption and legal fees mounted, John realized they couldn't afford to both make the trip. A young child would surely want his mother, he reasoned. So Julia reluctantly agreed to come alone.

Just a week ago, Angelina, a local translator and guide, had met her at the airport. After a sleepless night in Angelina's tiny apartment, they'd driven into the mountains to the small white orphanage teeming with children. The staff was kind, but had to care for so many with so few resources. They couldn't tell her much about Martin. He'd been left there as a baby and had grown into a quiet child who never made trouble. He befriended the cook, he liked to finger paint, and he mostly kept to himself.

Julia was shocked to learn a couple had come to adopt Martin a year ago. The next day, they had brought him back, saying they'd made a mistake. No other explanation was offered and the orphanage kept the fee. How could anyone return a child? He wasn't a coat with a missing button, but a young life worthy of loving care. She hoped Martin had been too young to remember this couple. Or did he remember them well and mistrust her, thinking she too would return him?

There was no bag to pack for Martin at the orphanage. He owned no clothes, no toys, no shoes. Not even a toothbrush. He climbed into the back seat of Angelina's tiny red car for the drive to her one bedroom apartment and wordlessly stared out the window as they drove down the narrow mountain road into the valley. Julia wondered how many times he'd been out of the orphanage in five years.

Martin didn't speak until they'd climbed the five flights to the apartment and saw a large meal Angelina's mother had prepared for them, laid out on the table. The boy excitedly piled his plate full of treats, asking about each dish, then quickly sat down and ate his fill.

While the adults conversed, with Angelina translating for Julia, Martin fell fast asleep at the table. Julia had carried him to a little cot in the bedroom, removed his sandals and tucked him in, kissing his forehead. Like a little cherub, she thought. Until the screams started in the dark.

Every night, Martin had nightmares, crying his heart out and she was helpless to stop them. She tried to hold and comfort him, but he pushed her away, crying harder until Angelina took the boy to her bed in the living room, whispering in his language, as Julia should have done, but couldn't. She'd paced anxiously until the boy fell back to sleep and she could carry him to his cot. While he slept, she'd stroke his hair gently, until he murmured, rolling away from her and she climbed back into bed.

Thud, thud, thud, thud. Thud, thud, thud, thud. Martin's short legs pumped as his cheap brown sandals slapped against the metal steps of the slide. Julia had brought a suitcase of new clothes for Martin but couldn't even get him to try on the bright red sneakers. He clung to the few things he owned. It was what he knew, all he had. Would he cling to his memories and be miserable in America? He would stand out there as much as she did here. Would the children in the school playground bully him? Was he shy and quiet because he was bullied in the orphanage? He was so small and so alone.

A tear started in the corner of her eye as she doubted her ability to mother this little stranger. He didn't even smell right to her. He was pungent, like cumin, foreign, alien.

Julia shook her head. *If only John were here, he'd know what to do,* she thought. She could hardly think in these mountains, the air was so thin. Julia was tired all the time, and the interrupted sleep each night made it worse. She'd tried to bond with Martin, but he didn't seem interested. Or maybe he just didn't know how. Or maybe she didn't. She was the youngest in the family and had never even had a babysitting job. What did she know about children, about mothering?

Climb, sit, slide, climb, sit, slide. The playground emptied as children were called upstairs by mothers hanging out the windows of the cheap concrete apartment buildings on either side of them. Julia's nose twitched inhaling delicious scents wafting from the windows, including the rich aroma of freshly baked bread. She'd have to herd the boy upstairs soon for the noontime meal Angelina was preparing. After lunch, they had another afternoon round of appointments with their lawyer, a doctor to certify the child's health and the passport office. There would be a few more pounds of paperwork to fill out.

Martin enjoyed the car ride to these offices, but retreated into frightened silence in the waiting rooms. Julia longed to hold him in her lap, hug him tightly and tell him she loved him, that it would be all right, but his body stiffened when she tried. He'd curl into himself, like a conch crawling into its protective spiral, and Julia couldn't break through the shell. After the appointments, she'd buy him ice cream and pastries, knowing she'd be rewarded with a smile between each sweet bite. How many times had he gone to bed with an empty belly?

The boy started up the ladder again. Julia wondered if he'd ever been able to get on the slide at the orphanage. Their playground had one slide, a few tire swings and two rough seesaws. With so many children vying for the equipment, perhaps this shy, quiet boy had rarely had the opportunity. Here he was king of the slide, and Julia smiled remembering how she felt so long ago when her mother took her to the playground. She'd loved the swings the best. Her mother would push her higher and higher, metal chain creaking, hair blowing back in the wind, flying, free of earthly bounds. Next she'd climb the slide, and Mom would be waiting at the bottom to catch, to protect, to love her. *That's what moms do.*

Getting up from the bench, Julia walked to the slide. They were alone on the playground. Martin's sandal hit the first rung of the ladder. Thud, thud, thud, thud. Julia crouched at the bottom of the slide. Thud, thud, thud, thud. Martin had reached the top of the ladder and was swinging his legs forward when he saw her. She grinned at him and held her arms wide open. He studied her as she waved her hands at him. "Come on, I'll catch you." She knew he couldn't understand her words, but he couldn't mistake her intent.

A slow smile spread across his face. He let go of the slide and slid into her arms. Julia picked him up and swung him and she heard him giggle. When she put him down, he ran to the ladder and started his climb, peeking at her from around the railing with every few steps. He peered at her from the top of the slide, swung his legs into place and waited. Julia crouched down at the bottom, opened her arms and Martin let go and glided to her. She picked him up and swung him again and he laughed.

Angelina called them from an upstairs window. Julia put Martin down and waved to acknowledge her. "We'll be right up," she shouted.

She turned to look for the boy, but he'd disappeared. Julia called him and he stuck his head out from under the slide. She pointed to Angelina's window. "Time to go up," she said. "Lunch." She made an eating motion and smiled.

Martin shook his head and ran to the ladder, slapping his sandals against the steps. Thud, thud, thud, thud. Thud, thud, thud, thud. He reached the top and grinned, sliding his legs to the front. It was their game now. She crouched down and opened her arms to him, opening her heart to this little stranger. Martin slid right in. Julia was his mother and she would always be there to catch him.

The stone's alive with what's invisible.
~ Seamus Heaney

Caving

For Eddy

By Laura Treacy Bentley

We walked to Laurel Cave,
had promised to go caving
if we survived
 a different
 kind of darkness.

It was sunny—a perfect autumn day
that made us think of spring.
We passed a wide-eyed girl
leaving the cave.
 She'd chickened out,
 left her boyfriend inside.

We wore old clothes
and a license to carry.
Underneath a rocky canopy,
shade eclipsed us as we glanced back
 at a jagged frame
 of sunlight and shadows.

Unafraid of caverns and the dark
you led the way.
I'd rather be hiking near a lake,
taking photographs of swans,
 but we had made a pact
 to come here.

When the last splinter of light
stitched shut behind us,
tiny bat hearts seem to pulse in my ears.
Incredible shrinking walls
 slowed our journey
 into endless night.

Barely room for my feet,
one foot tightroped behind the other,
I finally straddled a shallow stream
and became a human bridge,
 walking my hands on one side,
 wedging my feet tight to the other.

After my flashlight splashed
into our watery path,
your laughter diluted my fears.
You knew we'd make it out,
 had memorized
 the way.

Halfway in, we switched off our lights.
Newly blind, our disembodied voices
grew louder, then hushed.
I swear I heard that abandoned boyfriend cough
 and felt the blood
 leave my skin.

When a pinprick of sky widened,
I hurried toward a sky-blue exit
and thought I heard the chime
of a distant waterfall:
 the sun still shining,
 shadows still dancing.

Drenched with sweat and cave water,
I felt emboldened, euphoric, even proud.
"Are you ready to go back in?" you asked,
after we had rested a while.
 "You're kidding!" I said,
 thinking mission accomplished.

"That's our only choice—to go back in
the way we came. If we don't,
we'll be lost," you whispered.
I didn't feel so fearless anymore.
 Just a soggy Persephone
 in a faded sweatshirt,

holding a round-trip ticket to Hades.
Tired from willing myself
through the belly of a mountain,
I slowly surrendered
 and crawled back
 into lamp black winter.

The return trip went faster.
Surefooted this time,
I repeated my disappearing act
near sleeping bats on clammy rock walls
 and emerged even stronger, I think.
 No visible scars.

Sky Teacher

By Rob Merritt

Look at full sky in evening
and glimpse beyond
bombs and blasted dreams.

Rediscover Venus
above left of the new moon;
she moves higher every night
phasing lunar-like
toward crescent by February,
Mercury racing below
near the southern horizon
harder to see in the ever-later sunset.

Mercury passes the sun on the 20th;
Jupiter, low on the horizon like Mercury, on the 23rd—
the morning sky is filling up,
modeling for us
indefatigable energy
for circumnavigating a center of light.

We will pass through Saturn's rings this year.

May Venus increase your love,
and Mercury protect your travels.
May Diana encourage you toward the woods,
and Saturn give you justice and one good party before spring.

Jupiter offers you the sky.
Sunset January 31 will be twenty-five minutes later
than on January 1.

No matter how far apart,
we can bask in an ever-increasing light,
full, like the sky of winter.

Sago

By Susanna Holstein

Thunder and lightning darkened the day we buried my mother.
Icy gray rain mingled with salt tears and far away,
back home in West Virginia, other tears were falling
on the stormy earth in the mining community called Sago.

Thirteen miners were trapped in blackness deeper and yet still
in the same uncaring earth we dug to hold my mother's casket.
Thunder drowned our graveside sobs but even so we could hear
the keening cries of Sago.

Miraculous news awaited when we returned to my father's house.
The miners were rescued and everywhere, even in our house of sorrow,
people rejoiced. Some good had come on this dark day, it seemed.
The storm lifted, if only for a moment, to let the light shine through.

I will not forget the horror of the following hours,
of the terrible mistake. The miners, all except for one,
were dead. All of them, save one young man in critical condition.
Sadness swamped us. There was no miracle after all.

That night I lay in bed beside my father, who could not sleep alone
after sixty years of marriage. My tears soaked my mother's pillow.
Tears for her, for me, for men and families I did not know,
for my mother's life well-lived and for miners everywhere.

One and a half years later I journeyed to Sago,
to the memorial created for the lost miners,
to complete the circle of my mourning. But people were there,
and coal trucks from the Sago mine roared past, loaded with coal.

Arizona

By John N. Mugaas

December 7, 1941, 08:10 hours: Sweat-soaked and sick with dread, three levels below the forward deck of the USS Arizona, my crew and I labor in the powder magazine to supply our antiaircraft guns with ammunition. Amid the roar, chaos and our frantic haste, something soft caresses my neck and back. I pause. Time, like a brick of butter in a hot sauce pan, melts around me in a fiery yellow blur.

The apparition that touched me stands revealed, a vision of radiant beauty clothed in a rippling swirl of glittering robes. Her dazzling lapis lazuli eyes bathe me in cool light. Her hair is blacker than a raven's shadow; it ripples around her head and shoulders as if combed by the wind. Beautiful though she is, with a countenance exuding hope and solace, I am not ready for what she wants. But when she whispers my name, gentle as a lover's murmur, she is irresistible, and I yield to her outstretched arms. She takes me to her bosom, and while comforting me, she tenderly, oh, so tenderly, swaddles me in a soft fold of that eternal veil.

An irresistible force within the veil's gossamer fibers draws me out of the inanimate duff of my body and deposits the everlasting light of my being on its other side. There, I lie surrounded by a dim gray twilight.

I raise my head and look around. The sallow, indistinct forms of fellow sailors and marines lie scattered about me. We are floating just above the veil on something I cannot see. Fear grips me. I want to get away. I try to roll over or stand, but I am too weak. I cannot raise my arms. I close my eyes, ball my feeble hands into fists and scream.

The fit passes, but my fingers remain clenched. I open my eyes. A large luminous ball hovers over me. I gasp. To my horror, its translucent pale-yellow edge engulfs me. Its brilliant white center dissolves into me. I am aglow. I become buoyant and rise to my feet. My shipmates, already lucent, are standing. Their glow surrounds me.

I turn to one of them, but before I can speak, my eyes are drawn by telepathic command to a lustrous specter towering over us. A rainbow of shifting colors lightly clothes her torso. Her hair, ringlets of moonlight tumbling in a frolic around her neck and shoulders, frames a face noble as Lady Liberty's. The muscles in her arms and legs ripple with grace and power. In her right hand she wields a long thick shaft of green light, and an aura of authority surrounds her.

Her obsidian-black eyes capture mine. Tiny points of light in their depths probe and stroke my glowing core. When her eyes release me, my fingers relax.

I look around and whisper, "My God, we are so many."

The whole group is milling about and mingling. We greet one another and trade scraps of news about whom we have and have not seen. The need to know who is here drives us to assemble for roll call. I find my place. Below us, the surface of the veil reflects our collective incandescence; it gleams like polished pewter. Beyond the edge of our glow there is nothing but pale gray darkness. Fear, a tiny ravenous mouse, nibbles at my courage.

An officer intones the roll. Our chaplin keeps tally. Our names number 1,177. We are incredulous, but recall verifies it, and a soft buzz ripples through our ranks as we whisper the names of our missing shipmates, the survivors. And then we speak them, turning the buzz into a chant that becomes a shout, and each time our collective voices trumpet a name, a bolt of white light erupts from our midst, crashes into the veil and explodes into a blizzard of sparks.

A command from the specter stops our litany. She raises her shaft; its light pulses faster and faster until it glows with an unwavering green brilliance. Beneath our feet, a large portal opens in the surface of the veil and we look through it back into the world we had just left.

The battle of Pearl Harbor is over, but the chaos of its aftermath is in full rage. Within that appalling confusion, the portal, like the eye of an eagle, seeks the Arizona's 335 survivors. When each one comes into view, our whole cohort shouts his name, and, once again, a bolt of white light explodes from our midst. It flashes through the portal and is transformed into a slender silver thread that flies into our comrade's chest and coils around his heart.

From the wounded to the unscathed, their contorted faces reflect the depth of their grief and disbelief. I envy them their lives. Even the lives of the wounded seem better to me than this grim, dim, gray world. I want to hide, but where?

The parade of survivors ends. The great shaft dims. The portal closes. The specter lowers her arm.

Just as the wind dances with the face of the ocean, something invisible skitters from place to place across the veil, rippling its surface here, throwing it into billows there. This ceaseless, causeless motion unnerves me. My fear becomes a lion. With tooth and claw it shreds my courage. I break ranks and run. A clamor erupts around me. Grasping fingers slide off my shimmering surface. Where can I go? I don't know. Fear keeps me moving.

A telepathic command stops me. I turn toward the specter. She reaches into her bodice and pulls out a handful of glittering, multi-colored brilliance. It writhes and shimmers in her hand like a living thing struggling to break free. With a mighty heave, she casts the dazzling mass over us. I wrap my head in my arms and duck. The convulsing gob explodes into a shower of giant red embers; they plummet around us with a chaotic whoosh. The glowing brands settle onto the invisible substrate and coalesce into a glistening opaque veneer. Almost as quickly as it forms, this husk metamorphoses into a verdant layer of grass and flowers. Here and there clumps of trees and bushes uncoil from its surface. Like a ripple, it spreads rapidly outward, revealing an ever widening landscape bathed in pure, crystalline light.

Elated, my face and arms reach for the sky, and I turn, and turn, and turn. Breathless and dizzy, I pause to look. We are assembled on the flattened top of a hill. A valley with a small lake lies below us. Other hills extend for a great distance in every direction. One part of the horizon reveals a long sweep of soaring snow-capped mountains. The other shows off a span of red and white sandstone mesas that are cut into mazes by canyons full of deep blue shadows.

At last! Horizons define my location. Edges I can see mark the end of here and the beginning of there. There, a place of mystery, secrets and promises; it is a place begging to be explored. The distant craggy ridges and wind battered mountain tops sing to me.

A shout breaks my reverie. I look around. Halfway down the hillside my crew stands calling and waving, urging me to catch up. Below them, the rest of my shipmates move in a long meandering line toward the lake. Those leading reach the lake and wave vigorously to their fellows. Their voices, made small and indistinct by distance, are ripe with excitement.

My crew calls to me again, but I crave solitude and the sweet balm of the distant horizon. I wave them on. Weariness overcomes me. I sink to my knees, then lie on my back and gaze into the gleaming sky. It reminds me of the milk-glass coffee mugs clustered on my grandma's kitchen table, their translucent sides glowing in the early morning sun.

My thoughts turn to her. A pang of regret flashes through me. She is a strong woman who knows her Bible, and she quoted it often as she and Grandpa struggled to raise me. When I worried her beyond the limit of her strength, she would collapse into a chair, put her hands over her face, and say, "Oh sweet death, take me to your bosom."

"How did she know? How could anybody know?"

It will break her heart when she learns I got here first. She, who outlived her only child, my mother, will be crushed by the loss of her sole grandchild. Grandpa, who encouraged me to avoid the coal mines and enlist, will go for a long walk to be alone with his grief, to become accustomed to its fit before wearing it in public.

My friend from Montana, full of news and questions, comes to sit beside me. He has visited the lake, which he says is not a lake at all, but a crack in the landscape that reveals the veil. He walked around it and thinks it strange that there are no other creatures or people in this countryside. No wind either, yet that patch of veil continues to ripple and billow. No clouds. No water. How can there be so much light with no sun?

Finally, tired of his endless questions and speculations, I turn our talk to my grandma's tales of righteous rapture, salvation and the Kingdom. My friend met her once when he came home with me on leave to West Virginia. Afterward, on our way back to base, he had laughed and said, "Living with your grandma is like being on revival." But none of her stories fit. Our conversation stalls, and we join our fellows in the valley.

We discuss the specter and our curious surroundings. The desire to explore infects everyone; we become restless. Which horizon is closest? Many want to hike to the mountains. How long will that take? Others are drawn to the red and white mesas. What lies hidden there?

We disperse into the hills. Most venture out in groups of a dozen or more, but, others, like me and my friend, travel in pairs, and a few set off by themselves.

My friend and I choose as our goal a clustered trio of snow covered peaks, the tallest of the mountains. We start out at a fast pace, but our hike becomes a meander as we pause to examine each grove of trees, explore the base of every cliff and probe each coulee. Although we cross several hills and their intervening valleys, those cathedral-like peaks never get any closer.

We pick up our pace, determined to close the gap, when that rumbling telepathic voice interrupts. It strips us of our will and orders us back to the patch of veil we had so eagerly hiked away from.

We turn and retrace our steps. We are almost running when we top the first hill on our way back. The view on the other side is a paradox. It stops us. There, sparkling in the valley below is that patch of veil. Our shipmates stream out of the surrounding hills toward it, drawn like ants to a honey pot. Some are already in formation. We want to discuss this absurdity, but the urgent call hurries us on.

My friend and I slip into our places. The horizon, hills, grass, flowers and light vanish. The lustrous specter emerges from the gray twilight and steps into the orb of our glow. She points her green shaft to a quiet spot on the veil where soft living beams of light flow through. They bend, mingle and coalesce to form a dim recumbent figure. A gasp ripples through our ranks; it is one of our wounded shipmates. A luminous ball appears and merges with him. Aglow, he stands. The specter's eyes capture his for a moment, and then he turns to survey his surroundings. He sees our incandescence and stops. We cheer and clap. He blinks at us. A friend calls to him. Recognition and joy replace the confusion on his face. He hurries to our ranks and finds his spot.

The specter throws out a handful of glittering brilliance; light, verdant hills and the distant horizon replace the oppressive gray twilight.

Our chaplain urges us to remain in formation and worship with him. Not a few spurn the offer and hurry off into the hills, more determined than ever to reach the far horizon. During our worship, when we join hands in prayer, the intensity of our glow becomes a bonfire of love; our mission is revealed and accepted.

We have gathered at this patch of veil to greet 333 of our shipmates, and each time the dim recumbent figure merges with the luminous ball a cry of joy rips from my throat. But the dim gray twilight associated with these events still ignites a dreadful fear within me, and I can barely contain the urge to run. I find relief only when the specter regenerates light and those horizons of hope.

What of those who don't stay to pray after a shipmate joins us; those who are determined to escape the specter's call and overcome the paradox that cleaves us to this patch of veil? Well, even they are not immune to the sheer rapture of these events, and their number has dwindled, so when the 334th survivor joins us, and the chaplain calls us to worship, only one stubborn holdout walks away.

At last, the 335th survivor joins our ranks, and the specter, instead of restoring light, raises her shaft and opens the portal in the veil to reveal, lying just beneath the surface of Pearl Harbor's placid water, the sunken rusty hulk of the USS Arizona. Spanning her mid-section, just above the grasp of the tides, is a snow white structure. Its graceful upswept ends reach for the sky, and it appears to rise, like the Phoenix, from the destruction below.

The specter leads us through the portal. She points her shaft to one end of the structure, and we assemble there in a shrine hung with the solemn drapery of white marble. Each of us that perished in the hulk below finds our name graven, like a fresh wound, deep into the flesh of that stone. My fingers tremble as they trace the letters of my name.

The specter leads us out of that solemn shrine into the central ceremonial chamber. Sunlight, in dazzling fanfare, surges through graceful arching windows and overhead skylights. A group of sailors and marines, resplendent in their sharply creased uniforms, conduct the last stages of a ceremony. Sunlight sparkles and flashes from saber handles, rifles and gold braid.

One of the sailors carries a metal box in his gloved hands. A sob of joy bursts from the shipmate who just joined us. With slow measured steps, the sailor, followed by his riflemen, bugler, flag bearer, assembled civilians and us, carries the box from the ceremonial room, through the assembly and entry area, across the gangplank and onto the floating dock. A sigh sweeps through our ranks. Many of us weep.

A gust of wind ripples the water's surface, drawing our attention to the team of Navy divers treading water at the edge of the dock. The sailor halts before them, kneels, and hands one of them the box. The divers slip beneath the surface and so do we. The specter arranges us around an ugly gash in the Arizona's hull. The divers swim with slow dignity through our ranks and assemble there as well. We stand at attention and salute as the diver, with a graceful motion, releases the box into the void beneath that ghastly wound. After a respectful pause, the divers return to the floating dock. Their heads break the surface, and the riflemen fire their volleys.

Each blast propels us farther and farther away from this scene, back through the portal, back into our formation just above the veil. The portal closes, the specter restores the light, and we are thankful for the precious nugget of understanding now embedded in the glowing core of our being. The chaplain calls us to worship, and no one leaves our ranks. Afterwards, the horizons we have tried so hard to reach come to us, all of us.

New Choir Choice

By Ethan Fischer
(his last poem)

Soon perhaps
I shall join my voice
to the deep choir
thrilling underneath ground.
Our director knows
the soil shifts of music
and directs us down and up.
The audience has grown hungry,
but they stay for a while,
sensing a legend here
dying or being born.

Woodland Press, LLC

APPALACHIAN AUTHORS. APPALACHIAN STORIES.
APPALACHIAN PRIDE

Books Published In The USA
In Beautiful West Virginia

ATTENTION
RESELLERS / BOOKSTORES:
Stock Woodland Press Titles
By Contacting

Woodland Press, LLC

118 Woodland Drive, Suite 1101
CHAPMANVILLE, WV 25508

Bookstores, Writing Groups, and Retailers: If you would
like to order our catalog of book titles, or schedule a
Woodland Press author to appear at your book event,
contact us at email: woodlandpressllc@mac.com

OR CALL
(304) 752-7152
FAX (304) 752-9002

MEMBER

THE TALE OF THE DEVIL

NATIONAL BESTSELLER! Hardback. $24.95

Now own a piece of the feud. This handsome keepsake hardbound edition was used as source material in the recent HISTORY channel documentary, *America's Greatest Feud: Hatfields & McCoys*, directed by Mark Cowen and narrated by Kevin Costner. This book represents the first biography of Anderson "Devil Anse" Hatfield, meticulously researched and penned by the Devil's great-grandson, Dr. Coleman C. Hatfield, and Robert Y. Spence. A national bestseller.

Hardback.
330 Pages

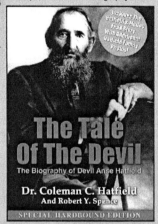

THE FEUDING HATFIELDS & McCOYS

NATIONAL BESTSELLER! $18.95

In this volume, you'll find a timeline of events that tracks the history of the Hatfield migration westward in broad strokes, and tells the rich American story of the Hatfield and McCoy feud. This national bestseller was used as source material in the HISTORY channel documentary, *America's Greatest Feud: Hatfields & McCoys*. It includes many feud-era photographs and family stories that have been passed down through the children of Anderson "Devil Anse" Hatfield.

Softcover. 192 pages.

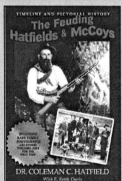

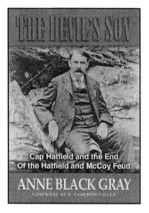

THE DEVIL'S SON

BESTSELLER! $21.95

The Hatfields & McCoys. You think you know who they were, why they fought, why they died. You know only the legend—now experience the real feud. *The Devil's Son* is a vast historical epic that breathes life into the individuals and families on either side of the Tug River. At the center of this novel is Cap Hatfield, son of Devil Anse, the seminal figure in the feud. While the battle rages, Cap wrestles with coming of age in the shadow of the Devil.

Softcover. 352 Pages.

Woodland Press, LLC

woodlandpress.com
(304) 752-7152
FAX (304) 752-9002
Email: woodlandpressllc@mac.com

MEMBER:

Edited by Michael Knost
Foreword by Rick Hautala

Legends of the Mountain State
Ghostly Tales from the State of West Virginia

LEGENDS VOL. 1

Softcover. $18.95

A powerful anthology featuring thirteen stories by master storytellers that will entertain readers as West Virginia makes a perfect setting for these ghostly tales and eerie happenings. Edited by Bram Stoker Award-Winner Michael Knost. 160 Pages.

Edited by Michael Knost
Foreword by Gov. Joe Manchin, III

"This is one excellent read."
Joe R. Lansdale

Legends of the Mountain State 2
More Ghostly Tales from the State of West Virginia

LEGENDS VOL. 2

Softcover. $14.95

This anthology embodies the same tone and texture of its forerunner, with 13 nationally known authors and storytellers sharing legends and ghost tales of the Mountain State. Each volume stands alone with bone-chilling tales from the mountains. 128 Pages

Edited by Michael Knost
Foreword by Homer Hickam

Legends of the Mountain State 3
More Ghostly Tales from the State of West Virginia

LEGENDS VOL. 3

Softcover. $18.95

Foreword by beloved American author, Homer Hickam. Regional myths and folklore provide the perfect archetypes for tales expressing the collective fears of the human race. This anthology offers more ghostly tales from the State of West Virginia. 144 Pages

Edited by Bram Stoker Award-winner
Michael Knost
Foreword by F. Keith Davis

Legends of the Mountain State 4
More Ghostly Tales from the State of West Virginia

LEGENDS VOL. 4

Softcover. $18.95

The fourth installment of the Legends series is here. Again, Appalachian myths, ghost tales, and folklore provide an eerie backdrop for powerful, dark, and gritty storytelling. Stories are penned by many of the preeminent writers in the horror industry today. 144 Pages.

Shadows and Mountains
FIRESIDE STORIES FROM THE DARK HEART OF APPALACHIA
Jessie Grayson
Ellen Thompson McCloud

SHADOWS & MOUNTAINS

Softcover. $13.95

Glimpse beyond the stunning beauty of Appalachia into what hides beneath. Allow these stories to guide you down spooky hollow roads and deep into the mysterious mountains within its dark heart, where monsters, mayhem and madness abound and things are never exactly as they seem. 140 Pages.

WRITERS WORKSHOP OF HORROR
Edited By
MICHAEL KNOST

WRITERS WORKSHOP

Softcover. $21.95

Edited by Michael Knost. This hit title was the winner of the 2009 International Bram Stoker Award, Superior Achievement in Non-fiction. Also, it was the winner of the 2009 Black Quill Award, Editor's Choice, Best Dark Genre Book of Non-Fiction. 262 Pages.